P9-DDA-711

THE NO. 2 FELINE DETECTIVE AGENCY

Center Point
Large Print

**This Large Print Book carries the
Seal of Approval of N.A.V.H.**

THE
No. 2 FELINE
DETECTIVE
AGENCY

MANDY MORTON

CENTER POINT LARGE PRINT
THORNDIKE, MAINE

This Center Point Large Print edition
is published in the year 2017 by arrangement with
St. Martin's Press.

Copyright © 2014 by Mandy Morton.

The text of this Large Print edition is unabridged.
In other aspects, this book may vary
from the original edition.
Printed in the United States of America
on permanent paper.
Set in 16-point Times New Roman type.

ISBN: 978-1-68324-416-5

Library of Congress Cataloging-in-Publication Data

Names: Morton, Mandy, author.
Title: The No. 2 Feline Detective Agency / Mandy Morton.
Description: Center Point Large Print edition. | Thorndike, Maine : Center Point Large Print, 2017. | Series: A Hettie Bagshot mystery ; 1
Identifiers: LCCN 2017009754 | ISBN 9781683244165
     (hardcover : alk. paper)
Subjects: LCSH: Cats—Fiction. | Large type books. | BISAC: FICTION / Mystery & Detective / Traditional British. | FICTION / Mystery & Detective / Women Sleuths. | GSAFD: Mystery fiction.
Classification: LCC PR6113.O8245 N6 2017b | DDC 823/.92—dc23
LC record available at https://lccn.loc.gov/2017009754

This book is dedicated to Hettie and Tilly,
two very fine cats, and to Nicola,
who shared the adventure

ACKNOWLEDGEMENTS

I would like to thank a small but perfectly formed band of people, who have helped to give life to this book: Nicola, for patience, solidarity and love; Neil Adcock and Debbie Barker for wrapping the book in such a glorious cardigan; Alexander McCall Smith, for his good-natured response to the title; Richard Reynolds, from Heffers in Cambridge, for his unshakeable faith; Susie Dunlop and all at Allison & Busby for giving a cat a good home; and Phyllis, for her encouragement and belief throughout.

CHAPTER ONE

Hettie Bagshot sat at her desk and stared at the phone, willing it to spring to life. The reporter's notepad and sharpened pencil sat unused by her right paw, and an un-mined drawer of business cards left no room for biscuits or other enticements. The reality of heading up a detective agency with nothing to detect was becoming a flea collar round her neck and—with the rent due on the Butters' back room—something had to be done.

Betty and Beryl Butter had run a very successful cake, pastry and pie shop for many years, and a chance discussion at their counter while Hettie waited for her 'usual'—a bacon and egg pie and a slice of Beryl's Madeira cake—had led to the back room and small garden shed being proffered for two pounds a week plus electricity. To Hettie's relief, the Butters had thrown in staff luncheon vouchers to complete the deal, but speaking of staff, where had Tilly got to? A pint of milk shouldn't be too hard to trace on a busy high street, and—in spite of her arthritis and vertically challenged tail—Tilly had proved to be an able assistant. And she was cheap. That, of course, was the main thing.

An unfamiliar noise made Hettie's elegant tabby fur stand on end, and it took her a moment to realise that the phone was actually working. Snatching up the receiver and trying not to panic, she stumbled out the words 'No. 2 Feline Detective Agency, Hettie Bagshot speaking,' completely forgetting to run through the list of options that she had trained Tilly to use as the official response to all potential clients. 'Yes,' she said brightly, 'we *do* look for cats who have gone missing. These cases can be tricky, though, and we rather prefer it if the missing cats are dead. That way they don't mind as much if it takes us a while to find them. Oh? They are dead? *Good.* Just one moment and I'll jot down some details.' Balancing the telephone receiver in one paw and reaching for her pencil and notepad with the other proved too much for Hettie: she, the pencil, the notepad and eventually the phone all slid across the desk onto the floor with a resounding crash. Remarkably, the caller was still hanging on when Hettie—now in the recovery position—resumed the conversation. 'I do apologise,' she said. 'The builders are with us this morning. We're refitting our offices to accommodate more staff, due to the recent demand on our services. Now, where were we?' Lying on the floor under her desk, Hettie realised that she had no idea who was on the end of the line. 'Shall I take some details?' she asked. 'You are?'

'Marcia Woolcoat, matron of the Furcross home for slightly older cats.'

Hettie scribbled the information down. 'You say the missing cats were dead before they left you? I see. And can you tell me how they died, as this may have a bearing on the case? They wanted to die? Why would they want to do that?' At this point, a pint of milk made its triumphant way through the door, hotly pursued by Tilly Jenkins, Hettie's not-so-able assistant. Seeing that there had been a bit of an incident in her absence, Tilly proceeded to the kettle in the hope that a welcome cup of tea could fix anything. Confused by the extraordinary story unfolding on the other end of the phone, and distracted by the thought of tea and a nice biscuit, Hettie arranged a 'face-to-face' for later that afternoon at Furcross. She replaced the receiver in time to rescue a landslide of custard creams from the staff sideboard, which Tilly had balanced too close to the edge. In fact, it was always thus with Tilly, and too close to the edge was fast becoming the mission statement for the No. 2 Feline Detective Agency.

CHAPTER TWO

Hettie missed the bus by a whisker, having paused to sample the latest creation from the Butters' autumn pie promotion as she passed through the shop and out into the September drizzle. She hated getting her fur wet and pulled up the collar on her best mac, cursing the bus as it moved away down the High Street. This was her big chance to pay her rent and put her detective agency up there with the professionals, and she had squandered it by getting too close to a salmon turnover. Brushing the final crumbs from the front of her mac, she had just resigned herself to a long walk when help arrived in the shape of a beaten-up twin-wheel base transit van, adorned with pipes and ladders and sporting a portrait of a tap dancing cat. The subtlety of the logo was lost on the community at large, but all knew the driver to be a very fine plumber—a cat who knew which end of a pipe the water came out of, and a grouter of high degree. Poppa Phene applied his brakes several times before finally coming to a standstill outside Oralia Claw's nail bar. 'Need a lift?' he shouted.

Hettie bustled forward, putting on her widest smile, and swung herself into the passenger seat, purring with appreciation. She had known Poppa for years, and they had shared a number of scrapes and difficult moments. Hettie had travelled far and wide in this very van during their rock band roadie days, she being the glamorous front of various musical ensembles and he her driver and the intermediary in any dispute that arose on tour. Hettie's music had been an acquired taste, a confused mix of folk, rock and country reggae, with an occasional nod to classical; her albums were favourably received, and had even become collectable as 'progressive acid rock'—whatever that meant. But she had realised long ago that there was no money in it, and her thirst for fame came second to her need to eat. Poppa had been her only constant companion on the musical rollercoaster, and they remained friends, living together for a while until Poppa's eating habits and Hettie's Virgo tendencies led to a certain amount of friction. But whenever the situation arose, they still made a handsome pair: a dapper short-haired black-and-white cat, with a curvy long-haired tabby on his arm.

'Do you know the Furcross home for slightly older cats?' Hettie asked, making herself comfortable. 'I need to be there in ten minutes.'

Poppa put his paw down and the transit jerked its way down the High Street, while Hettie struggled to release the handbrake that he had forgotten in his haste to please. Pussy Parton was coming to the end of one of her dead cat and Chevrolet songs on the van's radio as Poppa indicated left and turned right into Sheba Gardens. 'It's just up here,' he said. 'My old gran was in there for a bit. She made a few friends, then invited them all to live with her as one of those alternative lifestyle communes. They dressed themselves in lime green and grew their own catnip, but they got busted eventually.'

'For growing catnip?'

'No!' laughed Poppa. 'It was the lime green that went against them—that and the chanting. They were done for breaching the peace, but they got away with the catnip for personal use. Here we are. Shall I wait for you? I'm finished for the day.' Hettie wondered whether her arrival at Furcross in a plumber's van had been noticed by her potential client, and suggested that Poppa might like to wait for her out in Sheba Gardens, where she would come and find him later.

Furcross House was an old and somewhat dilapidated affair. Originally the town's maternity home, the building had stood empty and abandoned for many years until Marcia Woolcoat's numbers came up one Saturday night on *Scratch of the Day*. Hettie made her way up the drive, realising that her progress was observed by at least five pairs of eyes from the bay window to the left of the door, where a row of high wing-backed chairs contained a motley collection of elderly cats, all craning their necks in expectation. Hettie smoothed down her mac, only to discover that a half-eaten tuna melt had attached itself to the back during the ride in Poppa's van; there was no alternative but to stick it in her pocket and deal with it later.

Before she could knock, the door to Furcross was hurled open to reveal an overweight, over-dressed and overwrought ginger cat with at least three chins. 'Welcome to the Furcross home for slightly older cats, where twelve-plus is the new six. Marcia Woolcoat, at your service. Please come in.'

Before Miss Woolcoat had the chance to run through tariffs, menus and room availability, Hettie cut in and announced her purpose. 'Hettie Bagshot from the No. 2 Feline Detective Agency. You rang earlier about some missing residents.'

Deflated and a little embarrassed, Marcia took Hettie's mac—complete with tuna melt—and hung it on a peg by the door. 'Please come through to my parlour, where we can talk without disturbing my residents. It's been a very upsetting time. In fact, a number of them have felt the need to leave altogether, which is why I called you. My cook recommended you. She said you used to . . . er . . . hang out together in her rapper days—whatever that means. She's from Jamaica—came over on the Catrush with her family.'

By now Hettie knew exactly who her benefactor was. 'Marley Toke! I haven't seen her for years. I must catch up with her, but first tell me about your missing cats.'

Marcia Woolcoat sank into her fireside chair, offering Hettie the seat opposite, and began her tale of woe. 'At Furcross, we pride ourselves on offering every comfort to those cats who—for various reasons—wish to put themselves under our protective umbrella at a time in their lives when the outside world has become difficult. They arrive tired and worn out, off their food and occasionally suicidal. We cheer them up and give them nice meals—and if they really have had enough, we offer a special Dignicat service, complete with burial plot. Until recently, this was a facility that most residents signed up for as part of a special all-in package. We at Furcross believe that it is our absolute right to leave this earth in a manner, and at a time, of our own choosing. Society shuns older cats. It treats them as if they are only good for lying on cushions and dribbling, but here at Furcross we respect individuality and our residents are free to leave whenever they wish—as long as they pay up to the end of the month, and are happy to forfeit their deposit. In short, we are the utopia for the grey cat pound.'

Marcia Woolcoat was teetering on hysteria, and her mission statement had begun to overshadow the mystery that brought Hettie to her door. 'You mentioned that the missing cats were dead,' Hettie interjected firmly, bringing Marcia down from her conference platform. 'So I'm looking for their bodies?'

'Yes, I'm afraid you are—if you're willing to take the case. Before we go any further, I must know what your fee will be. With so many residents leaving us because of the . . . er . . . situation, and no real prospect of getting any new ones until matters are resolved, my coffers are running low—which is why I chose you. Marley told me that you were cheap and cheerful.'

Putting aside the professional slur on her reputation, Hettie remembered her urgent need to pay some rent to the Butters and swallowed what pride she had left. 'Well, I would naturally need to oversee the case and report directly to you,' she said, opening up negotiations, 'but I may need to bring in reinforcements from my agency employees, who are all carefully picked by me. My standard daily rate is two pounds, plus a further pound per extra pair of paws.' Seeing that Marcia Woolcoat showed no concern at the quoted price, and thinking she had pitched a little low, Hettie went in for the kill: 'Of course, there is a mileage charge and luncheon vouchers, and I may have to make several phone calls. It's surprising how many notebooks we get through, too.'

She made a mental note to tell Tilly to type up a rate card when she got back to the office; haggling devalued her sense of purpose. This was her very first job and she had absolutely no idea what to charge, but in bumping up the sundries she had misjudged Marcia Woolcoat's business head.

15

'Shall we say ten pounds per week to cover all costs, with the option of you and your operatives joining us for lunch and tea in our residents' dining room as and when? I will be happy to advance you the sum of three pounds on account.'

Realising she had been well and truly trounced, but knowing that the offer of three pounds up front would dig her out of her current financial crisis, Hettie agreed to the terms offered on the understanding that there would be a bonus of five pounds if she solved the case within a month. As she had no experience whatsoever of crime and her staff was non-existent, the chances of her solving the case at all were slim. But Hettie had always subscribed to the Micawber principle of something turning up—and wasn't that the first rule of detection?

The cats concluded their financial transaction, leaving Marcia Woolcoat's biscuit tin three pounds lighter and Hettie's tenancy at the Butters assured for another week. Miss Woolcoat struggled from her chair in a somewhat ungainly manner and led her new employee out of the parlour. 'The best way to explain the difficulties we are having here at Furcross is to show you what has occurred.' Hettie followed her into the hall and through what appeared to be the dining room, then out of some French windows to the back garden, which boasted a well-kept lawn, several scratching areas and a number of flower beds planted with geraniums

16

and cat mint. Straight ahead was a swing gate leading to another lawn, divided into small but tasteful burial plots, all sporting the 'in-house' style of headstone and Furcross logo—a reclining cat with a broad grin. Hettie found the logo a little disturbing, but said nothing as Marcia Woolcoat pushed on to the end of the most recent row. 'You see, this is what's happened: they've gone, three of our most recent Dignicat clients, fully paid-up and laid to rest, only to be dug up and stolen away without a trace.'

Hettie stared down at the three empty graves and wondered what she had taken on. It reminded her of Bert and Hair, the legendary body snatchers who stole corpses from graves and sold them to student vets and Chinese restaurants. She'd watched the film with Tilly only last week on their rental TV before a lack of funds forced them to send it back to the shop. 'This is a most distressing case. I think it best if you tell me about the events leading up to the discovery of the missing bodies. That will give me a clearer picture of what has occurred.' Hettie was pleased with her opening gambit and knew that she would get chapter and verse from Miss Woolcoat whether she wanted it or not. 'Shall we sit over there in the sun while you tell me all you know?'

Marcia Woolcoat sailed across the burial plots, coming to rest on a bench by the hedge. 'It was last Monday,' she began. 'Three of our top-of-the-range clients had booked their Dignicat procedures—or, as we like to call it, their final journeys—with our resident nurse, Alma ogadon. I should say at this point that a number of our clients prefer a group departure from this life. It makes their special day so much more pleasant and there really is a lovely atmosphere before they fall asleep. Those scheduled for departure were the misses Vita and Virginia—lifelong friends, if you know what I mean, and both still very beautiful. Vita was struggling with a nasty bug, and Virginia couldn't cope without her, so off they went together. The other client was Pansy Merlot, heiress to the Milgate bottling plant business. Pansy had become a little too fond of the family's endeavours and was drinking her way through her inheritance when she started seeing mice climbing the walls of her bedroom; as there were no mice, due to our strict rodent control policy, she decided to get off the bus, as she put it, before things got any worse. She was a top model before she embraced the bottling plant, I believe.'

Hettie found herself dozing off in the September sunshine, and only the thought of Poppa waiting patiently in Sheba Gardens kept her sufficiently alert to make the correct noises. Marcia Woolcoat battled on with her story. 'Once the procedure was complete, the bodies were prepared for burial by Nurse Mogadon. As they had signed up

18

for our five-star service, Oralia Claw, our local beautician, gave them a final makeover—hair, nails, jewellery, etcetera. The clients were then laid to rest in their bespoke caskets, surrounded by the little treasures that had meant so much to them in life. That, I might add, was an idea I came up with after visiting a Pharaoh cat's tomb on one of my educational forays into the unknown, and it serves the practical purpose of clearing away the old to make way for the new.' Hettie was getting used to Marcia Woolcoat's logic, and she had to admire her creative approach to getting rid of unwanted personal effects in readiness for new clients and their clutter. 'The open caskets were displayed in the dining room during lunch, when residents added small tokens of sustenance to equip the departed for their journey to the Elysian Fields. Then they were taken back to the departure suite, where they were screwed down and borne gently to the burial ground. The staff and residents gathered for a final farewell before Digger Patch filled them in, so to speak.'

'Digger Patch? Isn't he that old TV gardener turned romantic novelist?' interrupted Hettie, knowing he had been on Tilly's reading list for years.

'Yes, that's right. His publisher turned the last book down on grounds of obscenity, so he booked himself into Furcross on the under-standing that he would be in charge of the gardens

He helps out with all the burials, digs the graves and fills them in. He'smarvellous for his age. Anyway, where did I get to? Oh yes, after the graveside farewells we all trooped back to the dining room for tea, leaving Mr Patch to do the final interments. Marley had put on a lovely spread in accordance with Vita and Virginia's final wishes, and Marilyn Repel—one of the residents—gave a medley of show tunes on the piano. We were all cleared away and settled to the TV news by six.'

Hettie wondered if a blow-by-blow account of the average evening at Furcross was about to unfold, and headed Marcia Woolcoat off at the pass. 'Who discovered the bodies were missing, and when?'

'It was Tuesday lunchtime. Nola—that's Nola Ledge, our retired schoolmistress—was taking flowers to her sister Dolly's grave when she noticed the mounds of earth beside the new plots. It gave her such a turn that she ran slap bang into Digger Patch's wheelbarrow. I was summoned immediately, and after seeing for myself that the new graves were empty, I called the residents and staff together and ordered Marley Toke to serve lunch to give me time to decide what to do. By tea, one of our clients had left and two more were making arrangements to go, and Marley—seeing my distress—suggested I call you in.'

With all the talk of lunches and teas, Hettie realised that it was some time since she had put away the Butters' pie of the day. As the missing cats were already dead and tomorrow was another day, she could afford time to think before making her next move. Her head was full of questions, mostly about what Tilly had planned for their supper, and she took leave of Marcia Woolcoat, promising to return in the morning to talk to the residents. She collected her best work mac from the peg in the hallway, then made her way out to Sheba Gardens and the safe haven of the transit van.

Poppa listened as Hettie brought him up to speed on the first ever No. 2 Feline Detective Agency case, this time with the handbrake off. Having agreed to deliver her back to Furcross in the morning *en route* to a blocked sink, he dropped her in the High Street just as Oralia Claw was getting her board in. The Butters had shut up for the day and retired to their flat over the shop, so Hettie made her way down the side of the building to the back door, which opened onto the store-room and ovens and led eventually to her own rented office. Tilly worked a magic trick every evening, transforming the office into a cosy bedsit: Hettie's desk was now adorned with a slightly stained tablecloth and bowls and forks for two; the Butters' luncheon vouchers had been exchanged for a steak and kidney pie and a large packet of Salt & Shake crisps; and there was a saucer each of melted ice cream for pudding. As Hettie walked in, Tilly was just putting the finishing touches to the fire and laying out her blanket for later. Hettie's pipe and catnip pouch were on a small table by her chair, which had been dragged away from the filing cabinet and put centre stage in front of the grate, where a small but inviting collection of flames was coming to life.

Tilly looked up expectantly as Hettie hung her mac on the back of the door, and waited for the good news she'd spent the afternoon hoping for. She was not disappointed. 'Looks like the No. 2 Feline Detective Agency is in business,' said Hettie, trying hard not to skip round the room with sheer delight as Tilly offered a raw vocal soundtrack of 'We're in the Money'. She threw her bounty of three pounds down onto the dinner table, and the cats set about dividing the steak and kidney pie in half and breaking open the crisps; this proved a little more energetic than expected, but Tilly soon scooped them off the floor and into the bowls where they belonged.

The meal was soon over, and they retired to the comfort of the fire to enjoy their ice cream before getting down to the business of the day. With no real experience of detection, and no appetite for putting herself out, it dawned on Hettie somewhere between the second and third pipe of catnip that she had rather landed them in it: she had taken a case she had no idea how to solve, accepted money on account, and made an arrangement to return to the scene of the crime the next day to do whatever it was that detectives do. Bewildered and tired, she looked across at Tilly, who had been making copious notes as the case was outlined to her.

Tilly put her notepad down with some sort of resolution. 'It's quite simple really,' she said. 'It has to be an inside job, or someone close to one of the residents, or they wouldn't know who was dead and who wasn't. And if they weren't dead, then they wouldn't want them, would they?' Hettie was already lost but she tried to hang on as Tilly moved closer to the fire and continued. 'What we need to find out is if they wanted the cats who were dead or just the stuff they were dead with—and if that's the case, why didn't they leave the cats where they were and just take the stuff?' By now, Hettie felt obliged to make some sort of contribution to the conversation, but her head was spinning with Tilly's enthusiasm and there was no space for her to interject. 'This calls for a plan,' Tilly continued. 'We may have to set a trap. We need a plant.'

This was Hettie's moment. 'I'm not sure we should spend money on making the office look nice until we have a few more cases,' she observed cautiously as Tilly sucked the rubber off her new pencil and spat it into the fire. 'What sort of plant had you in mind?'

Refusing to follow Hettie's train of thought, Tilly pushed on with hers. 'This is a job for Jessie. Her charity shop's going through a rough patch and she's desperate for money. Could we run to another pair of paws?'

Hettie—more confused than ever but not surprised at the news that their old tabby friend's backstreet venture into retail would not be launched on the stock exchange any time soon—agreed to consider Jessie as a temporary recruit, provided there was good justification. A little late, the penny dropped. 'Oh I see! Jessie is to be planted at Furcross as an insider—brilliant! But can she be trusted not to lose her temper? She does have a bit of a reputation. We could end up being sued by Marcia Woolcoat.'

Tilly thought for a moment as she put the pan on for their bedtime milk. 'Do you think this Marcia Woolcoat can be trusted? She'd have to go along with Jessie being there. We couldn't afford to pay Furcross rates, and getting the TV back should be our first priority after the rent.'

Clearly they were both tired and the conversation was becoming more surreal by the secon . It was eventually agreed that Tilly would go to Furcross with Hettie in the morning, and would take notes during the questioning of residents and staff. The matter of their mole could wait until they had a better idea of what was going on—which, in Hettie's case, was a bit of a tall order. Delighted to be going further than the High Street, Tilly turned out the filing cabinet to look for her best cardigan while Hettie downed her hot milk, wound her alarm clock and curled up in her chair. It had been a long day, but there was no doubt that the No. 2 Feline Detective Agency was definitely on the map, even if the contour lines were a little shaky.

CHAPTER THREE

Tilly awoke as she always did to the firing up of the Butters' bread ovens. As she lay waiting for the warmth to permeate the walls of their room, she nuzzled each of her arthritic paws, encouraging them to face the day. She'd tried all the usual cures, but found that heat and nice dinners did more good than any nasty stuff in bottles. Since Hettie had taken her in, life was full of good food and warm beds, a great improvement on frosty old sheds and foraging in dustbins. Now, with their detective agency up and running, she actually had a sense of purpose in life—as well as organising and executing Hettie's every comfort, of course. With that in mind, she struggled from her blanket, folded it up and placed it in the filing cabinet for later, and put the kettle on for their morning tea. She padded softly round the room, reversing her evening ritual to transform bedsit into office again: the tablecloth was stowed in the bottom desk drawer; the dinner bowls—after a cursory wipe—were stacked in the fireplace; and the few stray crisps which still littered the carpet were tidied away as a breakfast starter. Licking the salt from her paws, and making some attempt to clean her face and ears at the same time, Tilly was now ready to coax Hettie into Thursday and

26

their appointment at the Furcross home for slightly older cats.

Hettie had been awake for some time, but preferred the chores to be concluded before she opened an eye or stretched a paw. Tilly was good at homemaking, and it would have been sinful to interfere with such a well-oiled machine before the first cup of tea had been delivered. The tea was hot, that was the best that could be said for it; this was the third day that the same teabag had been dangled into water and milk, but Tilly had conjured up a slice of bread with a scraping of cheese from somewhere, and they shared it before Hettie rose from her bed to start the day.

Feeling a little underfed, Hettie's heart leapt as she remembered Marcia Woolcoat's 'as and when' invitation to meals at Furcross. Pulling on her best mac, she made a mental note to string her interrogations out and make sure that she and Tilly were able to embrace every opportunity offered by Marley Toke's home cooking; Marley's jerk chicken had been legendary at rock festivals across the land in the days when Hettie and Poppa lurched from one summer gathering to another. Whilst Tilly buttoned her cardigan, Hettie took two pounds through to the Butters' shop to pay the rent and salivate over the prospects for dinner. Having exchanged their Thursday voucher for a lamb and leek pasty and one of Betty's extra cream doughnuts, Hettie collected Tilly, notepad and pencil and strode out with great purpose on to the High Street. They were just in time to see Poppa's van mount the pavement and come to a shuddering halt outside the post office, much to the annoyance of the elderly cats queuing to be first at the pension counter should Lavender Stamp, postmistress, feel inclined to unlock her doors and open for business.

With difficulty, Tilly climbed into the passenger seat of Poppa's van, getting a helpful shove from Hettie, who followed swiftly and slammed the door before Miss Stamp could unleash a tirade of abuse about pavements being for cats and roads being for motorised vehicles. Poppa took his time in forcing the van out into the traffic, making sure that Lavender got the full benefit of his exhaust pipe, and turned the radio up to drown out any further communication from the postmistress. Tilly found herself tapping along to one of her country music favourites, as Poppa and Hettie all but drowned out Tabby Wynette's version of 'Stand by your Van' with their own less tuneful but more energetic rendition. 'Oh, this takes me back,' sighed Hettie. 'The open road, driving to the sea to watch the sun come up, sleeping in the van, stealing milk from doorsteps and pushing on to the next happening, with giant jellies and as much catnip as a hubble bubble pipe would allow.'

Her raptures were rudely interrupted by a

radio newsflash: 'The bodies of three female cats have been discovered in the dumper bins at the back of Malkin and Sprinkle. If they belong to anyone listening, could those concerned fetch them immediately as they are a distraction from the department store's end of season sale. For the time being, the bodies have been moved to the haberdashery department; interested parties should contact Mr Sprinkle's office without delay. We now return to *Country Cats*, with the latest track from The Mavelicks.' Hettie was speechless. Poppa shut the radio off and swerved into the Cat and Fiddle's car park, and Tilly responded with a rare expletive. 'Bugger! They must be the missing cats. If they're found, we have no case, which means no TV and no teabags.' She had missed a trick in her panic, but Hettie was never short in rising to an occasion which had 'triumph' written all over it. Poppa read her mind and did what ended up being a seven-and-a-half-point turn, then headed back to the bottom of the High Street where the grand edifice of Malkin and Sprinkle had stood for over seventy years, offering everything a cat's heart could delight in: six floors of loveliness, from groceries to galoshes and—more recently, it would appear—a house of rest amid the buttons and ribbons.

'All we have to do is get the bodies back to Furcross and it's job done, plus a five-pound bonus into the bargain,' cried Hettie, throwing herself out of the van and dragging Tilly along by her cardigan. Poppa took advantage of a rare parking space and followed the girls into the store, only to find that he had arrived ahead of them due to a slight miscalculation on Hettie's part in exactly when to alight from the revolving doors. All present and correct, they took the escalator to the third floor and charged on through kittenware, toys and games, skidding to an ungainly three-cat pile-up in haberdashery, where a bespectacled Siamese cat patrolled her counter as if it were the Great Wall of China. Miss Lotus Ping, as her name tag suggested, was ready to call security, thinking that her department was under siege, but Hettie—putting on her most official voice and winning smile—calmed the situation by announcing their purpose. 'We've come for the bodies,' she said, as if asking for a yard of knicker elastic. 'They have been stolen from the Furcross Home for slightly older cats. My fellow operatives and I have come to collect them and return them safe and sound to their rightful resting places in their designated, state-of-the-art, futuristic, ecologically sound burial plots.' Tilly and Poppa felt there was nothing they could add, and hadn't a clue what Hettie was talking about anyway, so they stood by and waited for Miss Ping to get her head round the situation.

'You have to spleak wiv Mister Splinkle. I send for him to come quickerly.' Miss Ping dialled the manager's number, giving a brief overview of Hettie's mission. Within minutes, a silver-haired but bright-eyed gentleman cat, resplendent in a beautifully tailored three-piece suit and white carnation buttonhole, made his way to the counter. Miss Ping, overcome with emotion at sharing the same floor space, shrank back into her button cabinet.

'Hettie Bagshot from the No. 2 Feline Detective Agency,' said Hettie, pushing herself forward. 'I have come to claim the bodies you are storing here in haberdashery. They belong at the Furcross Home for . . .'

'Yes, yes, my dear, I'm sure you have,' interrupted Mr Sprinkle, 'but you need to have a look at them first, just to make sure they're the right ones. Miss Ping, kindly show our visitors into the storeroom. If the bodies prove satisfactory, we would appreciate immediate removal as they are attracting an unfortunate clientele. And Miss Ping—once Miss Bagshot has identified them, please see that they are nicely wrapped and ready for travel.' He turned back to Hettie and gave her a charming smile. 'Please excuse me. Mr Malkin and I have to inspect the final arrangements for our Autumn Fashion Event. We're lucky enough to be launching the new collection from Cocoa Repel, including her new fragrance. Make sure that Miss Ping gives you and your colleagues free dinner tickets for the evening before you leave

31

the store.' With that, Mr Sprinkle melted away into his shop like Santa Claus on Christmas Eve, leaving Hettie, Poppa and Tilly with the task of identifying three dead cats they had never even seen.

The bodies were laid side by side on a table normally used for measuring out bolts of material, and were respectfully covered in muslin. Miss Ping drew back the cover for Hettie to take a closer look. Three sweet, elderly faces appeared, peaceful and beautiful in death, but—on closer inspection—Hettie noticed that they had all undergone some form of shearing process; most of their body fur was missing. Not wishing to hold Poppa up from his blocked sink any longer, and knowing that the offer of lunch at Furcross would be off the menu if they didn't get a move on, she confirmed to Miss Ping that these were indeed the missing corpses and asked her to wrap them ready for transportation.

Poppa rearranged various pipes, toolboxes and—for some unknown reason—the front part of a vintage motorbike to fit the dead cats into the back of his van, all nicely parcelled up and secured with string and sealing wax. Miss Ping left her counter in haberdashery to wave them off, making sure that Hettie was also the proud owner of three tickets to Malkin and Sprinkle's fashion event of the year, and the twin-wheel base transit made its way down Sheba Gardens to Furcross House.

They parked in the driveway and Poppa sat with Tilly while Hettie made her way to the front door. Before she had a chance to use the knocker, the door was once again hurled open by Marcia Woolcoat, looking more than a little thunderous. 'Thank goodness you've finally arrived. I should tell you that I have a major rebellion on my paws. My residents and staff have been assembled in the dining room since breakfast, waiting to be interviewed. I have needlessly cancelled the Thursday morning country dance class; I've put off Oralia Claw's mobile nail bar until next week; Marley Toke is telling me that lunch will have to be cold cuts with Jamaican piccalilli, as she's left it too late to fire up the deep fat fryer; and Digger Patch is currently boring everyone to tears with a reading from his unpublished manuscript.'

Miss Woolcoat paused long enough to snatch a breath, which gave Hettie the window she needed. 'I do apologise, but there has been a major development in the case. My colleagues and I are delighted to be able to return to you the missing cats, and if Digger Patch would care to abandon his manuscript long enough to locate his wheelbarrow, we will transport them back to their burial plots and have them tucked up in time to help lay the tables for lunch.'

Marcia Woolcoat's overburdened lemon trouser suit threatened to burst at the seams, and her sigh of relief deadheaded the two tubs of roses that guarded the front door to Furcross. 'That is the best of news,' she gushed, 'and we have found their bespoke caskets at the back of Digger Patch's potting shed, so we won't need to run to the expense of new boxes. What luck we are having today! I'll be right back.'

With this, the chatelaine of Furcross blew down the hallway and disappeared into the dining room. Hettie returned to Poppa's van and waited for the unmistakable squeak of a wheelbarrow, followed by the gardening heart-throb and novelist, as he now liked to be known. Digger Patch was not so good-looking these days: his boyish face had become a little jowly—grumpy, even—and it was clear that his once famous whiskers had developed independent directions of their own. It occurred to Hettie that the producers of *Down Your Patch*, the show which had made his name, had been right not to consider a new contract; the downside of the decision was that the axed television star had found other ways of cashing in on his fame, unleashing a series of unfortunate literary disasters on an unsuspecting fan base. 'Miss Woolcoat says you needs the barrow,' mumbled Digger. 'I'd give you a hand but me back's bad, see—all them years turnin' the soil, cuttin' back, prunin' and the like, and I've a nasty sprain givin' me jip on me shoulder from diggin' up me Maris Pipers.' He paused, but the sympathy and recognition did not come so he pushed on. 'I expect you know who I am— the face of gardening since I was barely out of my kitten dungarees. Born with green paws and liquid fertiliser runnin' through me veins.'

Hettie nodded, trying to look interested. She dragged Tilly out of the van by her now over-stretched best cardigan, hoping that she might take the strain off Digger Patch's life story; at least Tilly would be pleased to meet the TV has-been, as she had read several of his books. Gently removing the wheelbarrow from Digger's iron grip, Hettie wheeled it to the back of the van where Poppa was waiting to load up Miss Ping's carefully wrapped parcels. 'I think we should leave them in the brown paper,' she whispered as he placed the last cat in the wheelbarrow, pleased to have fitted them all in.

'There's a side gate over there. I'll wheel 'em through that way,' Poppa said with a wink. He staggered across the drive, barging the gate open with the front of the wheelbarrow. One of the parcels dislodged itself and—in spite of Miss Ping's sealing wax—burst open to reveal a beautifully striped paw, pointing back in the direction of the van as if it preferred Malkin and Sprinkle. Hettie climbed across the barrow, which was now wedged in the gateway, and folded the paw back into the parcel. Straightening her best mac, she led Poppa and the wheelbarrow through the garden and on towards the burial plots. Marcia Woolcoat was waiting beside a rather odd-looking character with only one hind leg, the other having been replaced by a hand-carved stump; he sported an eye patch, too, and was dressed as if he had just arrived from the Napoleonic Wars or a perfor-mance of *HMS Pinafore*. The day had already established itself as some sort of horrific dream sequence, so Hettie decided to go with the flow and stepped forward to be introduced.

'This is Captain Silas Mariner, CBE,' puffed Marcia Woolcoat, as if the title made her as special as the Captain. 'He's one of our oldest and most distinguished residents. Miss Hettie Bagshot from the . . . er . . . No. 2 Feline Detective Agency. And who might you be?' Marcia asked, glaring at Poppa across the contents of Digger's wheel-barrow. 'Poppa Phene, sir,' responded Poppa, saluting the old sea cat and instantly currying favour. Silas lurched across to Hettie and kissed her paw in gallant fashion, casting his good eye across the parcels that lay forgotten in the exchange of social niceties.

Hettie noticed that three small but beautifully decorated coffins were lined up by the empty graves. Knowing that lunch would be served at any moment, she signalled to Poppa to park the wheelbarrow next to them, ready to reunite Vita, Virginia and Pansy with their chosen eternal overcoats. But there was, of course, a problem: Hettie had no idea who was who or who went where, and the only person who could help was Marcia Woolcoat. Summoning up the necessary courage and patience, Hettie cleared her throat and set about the most difficult task of the day so far. 'Miss Woolcoat, you may find this a little distressing but—as they are your clients—I wonder if you would be willing to sort the residents into the right caskets before we bury them? Unless you're happy for us to take pot luck? I should warn you that their bodies have lost some of their former glory, or to be more specific their fur, but they still have nice faces. We could unwrap the heads so you can have a quick . . .' Shocked, Marcia Woolcoat stepped back as if fleeing from an express train that was going to hit her anyway. The horror on her face was soon replaced by a substantial amount of Furcross mud, as she found herself prostrate and out for the count in Pansy Merlot's open grave, with two and a half pairs of eyes staring down at her.

'That's a bit of a sod,' said Poppa, while Hettie gasped at the thought of missing out on Marley Toke's cold cuts. 'I'll fetch a rope from the van and climb down there to get her out. We'll have to bring her round first to make sure she hasn't hurt herself. Best not to move her if she has—it could do more damage.'

Hettie responded by grabbing the watering can that lay by the hedge and emptying its contents into the grave, hoping to bring Marcia Woolcoat to her senses. The mix of cold water and liquid manure did the trick: bewildered, coughing and spluttering, and—in her current position—looking like the Bride of Dracula in a mud-splattered lemon trouser suit, Marcia Woolcoat grabbed at Poppa's rope and scrambled up the side of the grave. The assembled company tugged until her head finally appeared above ground, followed by a flailing collection of front and back legs, not necessarily in that order. Using the bottom of Hettie's best mac to pull herself up from the ground, Marcia Woolcoat rose to her full height minus her dignity, just as a bell sounded from the main building to summon the faithful to lunch.

The sea captain assisted Marcia Woolcoat across the lawn and through the French windows to the safety of her own parlour, away from prying eyes, while residents queued in a disorderly fashion for the dining room, waiting for Marley Toke to lift her hatch. Digger Patch had abandoned Tilly to be first in the queue, and she now joined Hettie and Poppa by the three dead cats at the burial ground. Taking control, if only briefly, Hettie made an effort to scrape the mud from the hem of her mac and randomly sorted the dead cat parcels into the caskets. Poppa screwed down the lids and tipped them one by one into the open graves. 'I think Digger Patch can fill them in, bad shoulder or not,' Hettie said, looking across the lawn towards the dining room. 'I've worked up quite an appetite with all this fresh air, and if we don't get a move on, they'll be onto seconds before we get a look in.' She strode away from the graves followed by Tilly, who was puzzling over the lack of 'stuff' in the coffins, and Poppa, who had quite forgotten about the blocked sink on the edge of town. A good plumber is worth waiting for, though, and Poppa had run his business entirely on that basis and on the principle of a free lunch whenever he could get one.

The dining room at Furcross was filling up by the time Hettie and Co. reached it, so Tilly was dispatched to bag a table while Hettie and Poppa made their approach on the canteen hatch. Before they even had a chance to take in the menu, a voice boomed out from behind a large vat of piccalilli.

'Stay where you are so's me can take a good, big look at you! Is it really Miss Hettie and dat Poppa boy, all de way from me travellin' days?' The voice belonged to a large black cat, wider than she was tall, who emerged waving a ladle as if she were conducting an orchestra. 'Oh my days! How you both doin'? I'm hearin' you turned detective, Lord take us,' said Marley Toke, pointing the ladle at Hettie and throwing a large

39

dollop of piccalilli down the front of her best mac, where it contrasted with the mud already drying nicely on the hem.

'Marley! I thought you'd gone back to Jamaica after the salmonella incident. I was so pleased when Marcia Woolcoat told me you worked here. It's been years, but you haven't changed a bit,' Hettie enthused as she held out her plate and Tilly's for Poppa to pile high with cold chicken and boiled ham. 'We must have a catch up when this case is over,' she promised, wanting to stay and chat but feeling the call of the feast that awaited her. Poppa, who was now concentrating on his own plate, passed up the offer of the piccalilli but invited Marley to chew over old times at the Cat and Fiddle at the weekend, recognising his chance to score some high-grade Jamaican catnip. The cook smoked it as part of her religion and sprinkled it into most of her dishes when no one was looking; her success on the festival circuit had been greater than most of the bands who performed, and her mobile smoking teepee was one of the most sought-after attractions at any three-day event—although after the first day very few could remember how the rest of it had gone. Poppa and Hettie both had fond memories of the time, although neither could quite access them.

Tilly had found a table by the window, and looked round at the eager band of residents tucking into Marley Toke's lunchtime offerings.

Those who had partaken of the Jamaican piccalilli were altogether more uplifted than the rest, she noticed, and, as the lunch progressed, a party atmosphere ensued, with one particular table bursting into song. It occurred to Tilly that had she not landed on her paws as Hettie's best friend and maid of all work, she would have been quite happy to spend her remaining days at Furcross.

Hettie and Poppa approached with laden plates, while most of the diners clambered back to Marley Toke's hatch to receive 'afters'.

'Lovely,' purred Hettie, springing into her chair and pulling her plate as close as she could to the edge of the table. Poppa, who had availed himself of several slices of bread, was busy making sandwiches by cramming as much cold meat into them as would decently fit.

'Why are you doing that?' Tilly asked, watching him wrap the sandwiches in paper napkins and deposit them in as many pockets as his work overalls allowed.

'It's an old roadie trick I learnt when I was on tour with the bands,' he explained through a mouthful of chicken. 'We were never too sure when we'd get to eat again, so if we landed a good canteen meal before the gig, we grabbed as much as we could for later. This cold meat is far too good for just one meal.' His trick started a chain reaction around the table, and Tilly followed suit by forcing several slices of boiled

41

ham into her cardigan pockets. Hettie, having eaten most of her plateful, eyed up the vegetarian option of cheese and biscuits which had been abandoned on the next table before reaching out and depositing it in her best mac pocket. The act of theft met with some resistance, as she discovered that this particular pocket already held the half eaten tuna melt from Poppa's van, now only fit for a desperate seagull. With sleight of paw, she swapped the cheese and biscuits for the tuna melt, leaving the offending and by now offensive item on the table just as Digger Patch returned with a large helping of Jamaican jam roly-poly, smothered in a flood of custard.

With the savoury foods either eaten or stowed away, Poppa went to pick up their puddings: Tilly preferring just custard—Jamaican or otherwise—and Hettie requiring lots of everything. When they were settled once again and the edge of Hettie's hunger had abated, their conversation finally turned to the Furcross mystery and what to do next. The Jamaican custard seemed to have inspired an upbeat and rather creative view of the case, especially from Hettie.

'Well, as far as I can see, it's case solved and no harm done. Marcia Woolcoat has her dead cats back and—with the three of us working the case—I reckon she owes us seven pounds plus a fiver for a quick result. I'm also going to put in for my mac to be dry-cleaned and a gallon of petrol for Poppa's van.'

Poppa smiled in agreement as he wiped the last of the custard off his chin, but Tilly shook her head in a troubled way which stopped Hettie in her tracks.

'The thing is,' she began, folding her napkin and adding it to the boiled ham in one of her cardigan pockets, 'we haven't really got to the bottom of it, have we? There are still questions to be answered. Who stole the dead cats in the first place? Why and how did they do it? Where is the stuff that was buried with them? And if they're not caught, will they do it again?'

'Well that's all sounding a bit difficult,' said Hettie. 'It's not like we're the bloody FBI or something. We wouldn't know where to start, and I don't think the Feline Bureau of Investigation would be interested anyway, so why should we worry? I think we should collect our fee and move on to the next case.'

Poppa felt that although he was not officially part of Hettie's latest business idea, he should add to the debate before things got awkward. 'If Marcia Whatsit just wanted the dead cats back, then everything's cool and we can move on— but if she asked you to solve the case, that's a different matter. By the sounds of it, you still have a way to go. Maybe you should go and have a word with her.'

Tilly nodded in agreement, but couldn't help adding one more question. 'What is our next case?'

Hettie—flustered and suffering a small bout of indigestion—shifted around the subject before admitting that there was at present no sign of another case. On that note, she set off towards Marcia Woolcoat's parlour to see how the land lay, leaving Poppa and Tilly to take a good look at the Furcross residents as they settled to their afternoon naps or recreations before tea.

Hettie found Marcia Woolcoat lying prostrate on her sofa with what looked like a damp tea towel across her eyes. The lemon trouser suit was a shadow of its former self and had been deposited on the floor by Marcia's well-stocked cocktail cabinet; instead, she was now swathed in a cerise housecoat, boasting puff sleeves and a neckline cut slightly too low. Her ginger fur stuck out in tufts through the gaps where front buttons just about hung on to her modesty, and Hettie was reminded of something that had inadvertently come ashore at Southwool one summer and had taken three tractors to return to the sea; in fact, it had put her off fish for a fort-night and she'd cashed in her tickets at Marine World for a cream tea and a round of clock golf. Wishing she had given the Jamaican custard a miss, she tried to focus on the reality of the current situation as the tea towel dropped from Marcia Woolcoat's forehead.

'Oh, Miss Bagshot! What is to be done? We at Furcross are not used to such nightmares during daylight hours. We have turned from a respectable home for slightly older cats into a moving picture set for *Shawn of the Dead.*' Hettie admired her choice of words, bearing in mind how little fur was left on the three dead residents. Slumped in the chair opposite, she let Miss Woolcoat continue while she tried to think of a plan of attack to implement when the tirad was finished. 'I fear that I am ruined. How can I ever live this down? No cat in their right mind would sign up to Furcross after this. I set out to provide a safe and comfortable haven—the best food, comfortable beds, elite outings, satellite television, an open house policy for visiting relatives, and a kind and humanitarian way out for those who wish it. And now it seems we are not even safe in our graves!'

The diatribe had been climbing in pitch for some time, and Hettie noticed that Marcia Woolcoat's fur had gone from ginger to a shade that matched her housecoat. It was not an attractive sight, and Hettie felt obliged to offer some form of consolation; there was no doubt that—in spite of the missing cats being returned—the case was far from over, as Tilly had pointed out.

Trying very hard to think of what a real detective might do, she stood and began to pace up and down between the cocktail cabinet and

45

Marcia's sofa; at least it felt decisive, and it must have looked good from where Marcia Woolcoat was attempting to sit up and adjust her fastenings. Taking a deep breath, Hettie said: 'Miss Woolcoat, my original plan was to speak with your residents to see if we could shed some light on what has happened here. That may sound disruptive, but I still feel it's a valid course of action.' Pleased with her phrasing so far, she continued: 'I am sure that those responsible will not try such a terrible thing again, but as a precaution I would like your permission to bring in a plant.'

Marcia Woolcoat looked thoughtful and responded in a measured way. 'Miss Bagshot, I'm afraid that is out of the question. As part of a contractual agreement, Digger Patch is responsible for anything green with a flower on it and . . .'

Hettie could see where this was heading and swung round on her heel, hitting Marcia Woolcoat full in the mouth with the belt of her best mac. Apologising, she tried to explain. 'No, no—a plant is a term we use for putting an operative into a place undercover. I have just the cat for the job. She will come to you as a new resident, keeping her eyes and ears open, and will report back to me on a daily basis.'

Marcia Woolcoat looked uneasy and a little confused. 'You're surely not suggesting that the grave robbers are here at Furcross, living among us? That is a very silly idea. Why would anyone want to do such a thing?'

Hettie was grateful not to have to answer the question. At that moment, Marley Toke burst through the door with a tray which she placed firmly in Marcia Woolcoat's lap. Clearly the deep fat fryer was back in action, as the tray boasted a large serving of Jamaican beer-battered fish and chips with a mountain of bread and butter and a large mug of steaming tea. 'Look what I done for you, Miss Marcie—it's yer favourite. Now come on, you'll waste clean away if you don't eat and dere's jam roly-poly for yer afters, wid me special custard.' Marley winked at this point, and Hettie began to muse over just how long it would take for Marcia Woolcoat actually to waste away— but it was the perfect time for her to take her leave and return to Poppa and Tilly. On the pretence of wishing to interview several of the other Furcross internees, she left the parlour to Marcia Woolcoat and her battered fish and made her way back to the dining room, arriving just in time for the pre-tea cabaret, led by screen icon and resident good-time girl Marilyn Repel, with her daughter Cocoa who had popped in for a visit.

Spotting Tilly over a sea of heads, Hettie made her way through the assembled company, none of whom turned a whisker at her approach as they sang and clapped their way through some almost recognisable show tunes. Captain Silas

47

was attempting a one-legged hornpipe, while the old retired schoolmistress, Nola Ledge, kept pace by knitting in time to a selection of random notes pounded out by Nutty Slack, the chimney sweep. Nutty was a regular afternoon visitor and particularly sweet on Nola, who avoided his advances but knitted him winter jumpers and shared a table with him most afternoons at tea; since her sister Dolly passed away, Nola had been lonely and Nutty made her laugh with his merry quips and over-the-top waistcoats. And for a chimney sweep, he was very clean.

The centrepiece of the entertainment, though, was a vivacious siren of a cat who still dyed all her visible hair blonde in memory of the many movies she had made. There was no doubt that even now, in her twilight years, Marilyn Repel could turn heads with her flashing eyes and pearl white teeth. Her voice, however, had passed its sell-by date by the time she made *The Prince and the Showcat*, a romantic comedy with Irish theatre star Larry O'Liver. Both of them had bitten off more than they could chew, with Marilyn constantly turning up late on set and Larry hardly ever turning up at all; the film was eventually released as a pornographic thriller, which surprised the critics and shocked anyone who was unfortunate enough to see it. Afterwards, Larry went back to the stage and Marilyn found herself in great demand as a cabaret artist in the

Parisian red light district; there, she met, married and buried a French cat called Surge Forward—but not before she had borne him a daughter. Cocoa Repel had grown up to become one of the world's most innovative patrons of Hoot Cature and, more recently, had founded her own perfume house at the back of Oralia Claw's nail bar. With her mother's vast fortune to prop up any little idea that occurred to her, she was on the up and a force to be reckoned with. Now, she broke away from the teatime warm up session to pass among the Furcross audience with flyers, and as Hettie made her way through the throng, Cocoa slapped one firmly on the chest of her best mac, where it attached itself to the dollop of piccalilli deposited earlier by Marley Toke.

'What a nightmare!' Hettie spluttered to Tilly, having had the best part of an alcoholic ginger beer tipped over her by Digger Patch as he swayed to the dying moments of 'Diamonds are a Cat's Best Friend'. 'There doesn't seem to be any point in trying to talk to anyone here today: Marcia Woolcoat isn't up for your plant, and is currently being devoured by a beer-battered fish; Marley Toke has laced the rest of the residents with catnip, and God knows what state they'll be in by the time they've eaten their tea. I doubt that any of them could remember what happened on Monday when Vita, Virginia and Pansy were buried. Speaking of burials, has anyone been to fill them in yet? Now they're back, the least someone could do is chuck some soil on them.'

Tilly could see that her friend had 'lost it', as Poppa would say, and led Hettie by the paw into the Furcross lounge. It was much quieter there, with only one resident fast asleep in front of the TV set that dominated the room. The cat was small and petite, with a very attractive pink and grey stripe running through her fur, and her uniform marked her out as Alma Mogadon, the Furcross nurse. Tilly had become a little overexcited at the scale and size of the TV, and in her enthusiasm to take a closer look, she tripped over Alma's legs—but Nurse Alma Mogadon did not wake up. In fact, Nurse Alma Mogadon was never going to wake up, because Nurse Alma Mogadon was dead.

'Well, that's all we need,' said Hettie, slumping into the chair next to the late nurse as Tilly fiddled with the TV remote. 'Four corpses in one day, and still no closer to the truth of it. You'd think—being a nurse—she could look after herself instead of adding to the body count.'

'I don't suppose she's done it on purpose,' offered Tilly, trying to work out how to bring the TV screen to life. 'Look—there's a letter sticking out of her apron pocket. That might be important.'

Feeling irritated and more than a little waspish because of her indigestion, Hettie snatched the

50

letter from the body. ' "Marcie." That's what it says. Probably a note for Miss Woolcoat. Nothing to do with us, anyway. I'll stick it back in her pocket. We've got enough on without running an after-death postal delivery service, and it's getting late—time we were heading off for the day. Where's Poppa?'

'He's gone to sort his blocked sink out, and he's picking us up on the way back. Shouldn't we tell someone about the nurse? Miss Woolcoat will have to deal with it. That body can't just stay there while they all watch TV later. It doesn't seem right, and it's bound to take the edge off their enjoyment of the six o'clock news.'

'Judging by the state they're in, I doubt they would even notice,' grumbled Hettie as she looked at the corpse more intently. 'I'd say it was a peaceful death. Nothing suspicious, no signs of violence, and—looking on the bright side—one less for us to interview before we wrap the case up.'

Tilly had given up with the remote control. Defeated by technology, she turned her attention to the letter that Hettie had seen fit to ignore. Opening the envelope, she read the enclosed note out loud:

My dear Marcie,
Please forgive me for taking a coward's way out, but I cannot live with what I

51

have done, and I hope that Pansy, Vita and Virginia can forgive me for allowing it to happen to them. Goodbye, with love.

Alma x

'See—I told you it might be important. It's a confession,' said Tilly, looking like the cat who had most certainly got the cream. 'She's killed herself before anyone could find out what she did. Bit sad, really, but I don't see how she did it all on her own. I don't think we've quite got to the bottom of it yet.'

Just as Hettie was about to launch herself into an appraisal of the facts so far, the lounge door crashed open to reveal a laden tea trolley, propelled by Marley Toke. The shock afforded to the trolley by the sheer speed as it hit the skirting board *en route* dislodged a plateful of Chelsea buns, sending one spinning towards Tilly's head. As she ducked, the offending item hit the TV screen and slid down towards the standby button, which responded by coming to life to reveal a full colour image of the folk singer Ralph McTail in concert—much to Tilly's delight and Marley's embarrassment. The only person unmoved by the sudden arrival of afternoon tea was Nurse Alma Mogadon, who sat passively with one of the stray teatime treats lodged firmly in her crisp, white nurse's cap.

'Me thought you'd like yer tea in 'ere, away

from de stampede, Miss Hettie—but me trolley wheels don't seem to go de same way as me these days. The Lord be praised that me samovar kept its place on de top deck, or we'd be paddlin' around in Jamaican Darjeeling and . . .' The sentence came to an abrupt halt, unlike the tea trolley which continued its journey across the floor, finally settling against a rattan bookshelf. 'Nurse Moggy! Whatever is you doin' sat dere like a statue with one of me sticky buns on yer head?'

With no response forthcoming, Hettie gently intervened. 'I'm afraid she's dead, Marley. She appears to have killed herself.'

'Dead! What is you sayin'? How can she be dead? She was alive this mornin', so how can she be dead now? She's a nurse—that don't make any sense! She always come to cash and carry wid me on Friday, so she wouldn't just die and not tell me, and we got tickets for Miss Repel's fashion show on Saturday, and we booked us a week at the Signet Hotel in Southwool for de Festival in November. Me and Moggy always has a week at the seaside before Christmas.

Running out of calendar dates, Marley sank into the chair on the other side of the deceased nurse and began to rock backwards and forwards. As she lapsedinto a trance-like state, a low and tuneful hum escaped from her reverberating lips and herlarge, hooped earrings swung in time to the rhythmic rocking of her substantial body.

The scene was one of those tableaux that could only have been created by a seriously deranged experimental theatre director, and Tilly realised that it was time to bring the curtain down before any of the Furcross residents added to the confusion. Finding the off button on the TV remote, she took control. 'Right—we have to remove the body before anyone turns up.' Looking across at Marley and remembering a scene from *Voodoo Cats*, she knew that trance-like states should not be tampered with, but Hettie would need spurring into action if the dead nurse's dignity was not to suffer any further humiliation. 'Fetch the trolley. We'll load her up and take her to Marcia Woolcoat's parlour. She can deal with it after that.'

Hettie responded immediately, grateful to her friend for making some attempt to extricate them from yet another off-colour moment at Furcross. As if Marley's humming—which now evolved into a chant—had summoned the cavalry over the sand dunes, Poppa made a *Lawrence of Arabia* entrance just when they needed him most. Surveying the scene, but showing no real surprise, he sprang to Hettie's aid and they lifted Nurse Mogadon out of her chair, squeezing her onto the bottom layer of the tea trolley. Tilly collected the scattered buns, remembering to conceal three in her now bulging cardigan

54

pockets for later. Scanning the room, she located a tartan blanket nestling in one of the armchairs and tucked it as best she could around the body on the trolley, preparing it for departure. Satisfied that the lounge was back to normal except for the wailing Jamaican cook, and with a lingering look at the oversized TV, Tilly led the way, opening doors as Hettie and Poppa attempted to steer the tea trolley into the hallway and down the corridor to Marcia Woolcoat's parlour.

Marley Toke's Jamaican beer-battered fish and chips had proved a real tonic, and Marcia Woolcoat responded brightly to the polite knock at her door. As the funeral cortège rattled into her parlour, complete with samovar and Chelsea buns, she fidgeted nervously, eyeing up the tartan blanket and wondering why her Jamaican cook—whom she paid far too well—had not delivered her afternoon tea personally. 'Miss Bagshot and . . . er . . . your associates—this is a surprise. What news do you bring? Are you any closer to getting to the bottom of this dreadful business? I must apologise for my state of mind earlier, but it's not every day that you are called upon to identify three bodies and subsequently find yourself prostrate in a grave, especially when you are very much alive. I fear my nerves got the better of me. Shall we have some tea and discuss your progress?'

Tilly moved first and put the suicide note into

Hettie's paw, giving her a meaningful stare and nudging her towards Marcia Woolcoat. Adjusting her mac and raising herself to her full height, Hettie assumed the stance of someone in authority who had everything under control—much to the admiration of her two friends, who had put the tea trolley between themselves and the matron of Furcross. 'Miss Woolcoat, I'm afraid the news continues to be bad. In spite of our endeavours to find the perpetrator behind your . . . er . . . problems here at Furcross, it would appear that the . . . er . . . plot thickens. There has been a death which—although it appears to be voluntary— is not part of your Dignicat scheme.'

Hettie could not resist turning her head towards the bottom layer of the trolley as the word 'scheme' died in her throat. Marcia followed her gaze and mentally converted the tartan bundle into her worst fears. She let out a piercing scream and fell back on her sofa, her ginger fur becoming spiked and greasy in seconds. 'Please! Not Marley!' she cried as the sobs got louder. 'Who's going to cook for us? No one could make the housekeeping money go as far as Marley Toke—she has friends in low places. We are done for! I am done for!'

Hettie allowed the performance to reach a crescendo before shaking the queen of melodrama out of her 'in the moment' approach, and handing her the cup of sweet tea that Tilly had coaxed from the samovar. Amid sobs and loud slurps, Marcia Woolcoat gradually regained a grain of composure and Hettie grasped the moment to slip the letter into her tear-soaked paws. Retreating behind the tea trolley to join her friends, she watched as Marcia Woolcoat unfolded Alma Mogadon's final words.

As the contents began to sink in, Marcia visibly became a very old cat. Her haughty demeanour melted away, and was replaced by a sad, dejected picture of her original self. There were no more tears and no sign of any earth-shattering sobs, just a silent resignation. She rose from her sofa and slowly approached the tartan bundle, pulling back the cover to reveal a familiar face, now still and frozen in time. It was as if the onlookers had no physical presence in the room as she pulled the nurse's body to her, releasing it from the trolley. Kneeling down, she cradled Alma's head in her lap and began to speak softly, her words clearly an intimate, one-sided conversation.

Out of respect for Marcia's grief, Hettie allowed her gaze to wander round the room, only to appreciate for the first time how many elaborately framed photographs captured the image of Alma Mogadon—arm in arm with Marcia on a beach, curled up on a picnic rug, or posed in front of some well-known monument, but always smiling: two cats delighting in each other's company. Offering a conspiratorial nod to Poppa and a quick tug of Tilly's cardigan, Hettie led the way towards the door, leaving the room with as little ceremony as she could.

No sooner were they back in the corridor than the full impact of Marley Toke's continuous wailing made Hettie's mind up: there was nothing more to be done today. The thought of a roaring fire, a pipe or two of catnip and one of the Butters' finest lamb and leek pasties suddenly lifted her spirits, and with a spring in her step she led her party to the safety of Poppa's van. In his haste, he had abandoned the vehicle across the driveway entrance to Furcross, much to the annoyance of Oralia Claw, who was jamming her paw down on the horn of her mobile nail bar, obviously desperate to gain admittance. Much shoving and shunting eventually resolved the situation, and Poppa steered the transit out into Sheba Gardens. By way of celebration at having escaped the mausoleum that Furcross was fast becoming, Tilly dug out the Chelsea buns from her cardigan and shared them out, and all three offered backing vocals to Steponcat's 'Born to be Mild', featured as the regular thrash metal spot on their local radio's Drive-time Show.

'I'm not sure where any of this leaves us,' observed Hettie, picking a stray currant off Poppa's windscreen. 'Four dead cats, three of them half-skinned and one of them confessing to God knows what in connection with the other three; a home full of barking mad elderly cats; a cook in some sort of Voodoo trance; and Marcia Woolcoat in no condition to settle up for as much as a paper clip.'

'It's a bit of a bugger,' agreed Tilly. 'We might have bitten off more than we can chew. Maybe we should quit while we're losing and go on to the next case.'

'Yes, but that's the point—we don't have another case to go on to. I don't see what choice we have but to push on and try and make sense of it all. We obviously need a plan.'

'Well, for a start we need teabags,' piped up Tilly, doing her best to be positive.

'My shout.' Poppa shot through a set of red lights, bringing the transit to a shuddering halt outside the entrance to Malkin and Sprinkle's food hall. 'I've got to get a pie for tea anyway, and the Butters will have shut by now. Keep an eye on the van. I'll be back in a tick.'

He forced the driver's door open into a crowd of unsuspecting shoppers and headed for the grocery department. Hettie noticed that a ham sandwich had made its bid for freedom from one of his overall pockets, and she was about to retrieve it from the pavement when Oralia Claw's nail van loomed out of nowhere, mounting the pavement and squashing the sandwich under one of its front wheels. The destruction of the sandwich was eclipsed by Cocoa Repel's ungainly exit from Oralia's passenger seat, at which point a small crowd gathered, proffering bits of paper and anything else they could find to carry off the designer's signature. Hettie instantly adopted her surveillance position, glancing into the rear-view mirror until Tilly gently pointed out that all the action was taking place in front of them, and they watched, transfixed, as the sleek, beautiful chocolate cat draped herself across the bonnet of the van, chatting to her public and giving out eaflets for her big event. Under the weight of boxes and rails full of Cocoa Repel's latest collection, Oralia Claw staggered from the back of her van to the trade entrance of Malkin and Sprinkle. Unlike her companion, Oralia had to work at being beautiful: her pinched, black-and-white striped face and thin, under-developed body gave her a snake-like appearance, but her nails were immaculate and her fur shone like glass.

Oralia Claw had fallen on her paws the day she met Cocoa Repel at Furcross. Cocoa had dropped in on the off chance that her retired movie star mother would smile financially on her latest scheme, and had that afternoon walked away with a merger that suited all concerned. Oralia had taken care of Marilyn Repel's fur and nails for some time, and her weekly visits to Furcross were much looked forward to, especially since she had branched out into the world of accessories and was now able to tempt her clients with leg warmers, hats, gloves and handbags, as well as established beauty treatments. She had converted an old garage at the rear of her premises in the High Street and, on quiet days, would close her shop and take herself off to what she liked to call her 'back place' to 'knock up a bit of stock'.

Cocoa Repel had built up a very successful fashion emporium on the east coast, mostly due to the constant flow of her mother's fortune. On the day she met Oralia, she had been looking to expand her options into 'off-the-peg, one-size-fits-all' couture, and the two had swapped visions over a pot of Marley Toke's Jamaican coffee. In the end, Oralia agreed to extend her 'back place' to accommodate Cocoa's new design studio and perfumery, and was offered in exchange the chance to feature her own handiwork at some exclusive fashion events.

It was obvious to any onlooker that Cocoa wore the leg warmers in this particular venture, and that Oralia—still staggering under the burden of Saturday evening's extravaganza—was not so much the silent partner as the put-up and shut-up end of the business. The Malkin and Sprinkle event was the pinnacle of Oralia Claw's achievements so far and, as a gust of wind picked her and the large box she was carrying up into the air, dashing them both against the department store's electrical and homeware window, she had no choice but to accept that there was no gain without pain.

Hettie and Tilly did their best to suppress peals of laughter as the comedy unfolded in front of them, along with an assortment of chiffon scarves that had escaped from the crumpled box and wrapped themselves around lamp posts and passers-by. Cocoa managed to disengage herself from her fan base and totter on overambitious heels to where Oralia lay sprawled on the pavement; she made encouraging noises but offered no physical support, and Poppa emerged from the food hall just in time to pick up the pieces. Abandoning his shopping, he hauled the nail bar hostess to her feet while a large gathering of shoppers danced round the box, trying to catch what was left of its contents.

'It's just like watching one of those contemporary dance things,' observed Tilly, wiping tears from her eyes. 'You know the sort of thing—lots of leaping about in coloured tights and floaty things with no one in the audience knowing when to clap.'

'More like the dying swan from where I'm sitting,' Hettie said.

Poppa extricated himself from the ongoing situation, rescued his shopping and climbed back into the transit as both Mr Malkin and Mr Sprinkle appeared on the pavement to add to the commotion, accompanied by Lotus Ping and the store's first-aid box.

'Blimey!' he said, tossing the biggest box of

teabags he could find over to Tilly. 'It's worse than the artists' bar on Folk Festival Sunday out there. I think we should turn up for this show on Saturday. It promises to be the gig of the century, and we've got free tickets to a sit-down dinner before the cabaret starts. If Oralia Claw's doing the choreography, that's bound to be a winner.'

Leaving the chaos behind, Poppa drove Hettie and Tilly home and arranged to pick them up the following morning for a 'see how the land lies' visit to Furcross. The three friends were tired and hungry. In spite of the recent merriment, the day had been a difficult one—and, for Nurse Mogadon and Marcia Woolcoat, a very sad one. Hettie knew that they were no closer to solving the case, if there had ever been a case in the first place, and Tilly was right: it had to be an inside job, especially now that there was a confession of sorts from the nurse in charge of dispatching the missing cats. And what was Marcia Woolcoat's role in all this? Perhaps tomorrow would supply some long-overdue answers, not to mention a hard cash payment for services so far rendered; in the meantime, there was a hearty supper and a warm fire to look forward to, and Hettie satisfied herself that the day would end far better than it had begun. Unless you were Nurse Mogadon, of course.

CHAPTER FOUR

The fire had died down long before the hammering began, and it was Tilly's urgent tugging at her blanket that finally woke Hettie from a dream in which a giant chicken pie was about to eat her. 'Whatever is the matter?' she snapped as the hammering got louder.

'There's someone at the back door,' said Tilly, dragging Hettie's blanket off her and forcing a dressing gown into her stomach. 'You'll have to go or the noise will wake the Butters and we'll be out on our ear. It's three o'clock in the morning. Hurry up!'

Hettie threw her dressing gown on with very little ceremony and lurched towards the door, kicking what was left of her milky bedtime drink down the front of Tilly's pyjamas. As she hurried along the corridor to the source of the hammering, a light illuminated the Butters' staircase and the sisters appeared on the top landing in matching monogrammed nylon nighties, their long hair restricted by a battalion of curlers and grips. 'Don't worry!' she shouted up the stairs, seeing the alarm on her landladies' faces. 'I'm . . . er . . . expecting a parcel.'

She congratulated herself for her quick thinking as the Butters shuffled back into their flat, unconvinced but satisfied that the assault on their back door would soon be over. The hammering continued, and Hettie hurled the door open so suddenly that the final blow hit her squarely on the chin. Marley Toke—soaked from the overnight rain—fell over the threshold. The momentum—and Marley's weight—propelled the two cats backwards, crushing Tilly who was using Hettie as a deflector shield against the unknown caller. Marley hauled herself up to allow Hettie enough room to get to her feet, and the bundle of wet cat fur eventually sorted itself out. Tilly, a little shaken, crawled away from the scrum to lick her arthritic paws.

Leading the way back to their room, Hettie shut the door, relieved to return to the privacy and sanctuary of home. Tilly, still rubbing one of her paws, put the kettle on and offered Marley her own blanket, as Hettie encouraged the fire into life with a violent prod and a few small bits of coal. Grateful for the warmth and too upset to speak, Marley sobbed quietly by the fire while Tilly poured hot tea into three mugs, and Hettie—realising there were issues to address—ransacked Tilly's cardigan pockets and her own best mac for the ham, cheese and biscuits procured from the Furcross dining room. It seemed a very long time ago now, but the ham had held up well and the cheese was recognisable; only the biscuits were shadows of their former selves. As luck would have it, Hettie spotted a number of unclaimed custard creams under the staff sideboard and blew the dust off before adding them to the impromptu feast.

Tilly's hot tea revived Marley's spirits in no time. As the flames began to climb up the chimney breast, her sobs subsided and the three cats stared into the fire, waiting for the revelations to begin. With nothing forthcoming, Hettie reached for a slice of ham and folded it into her mouth. Tilly was making inroads into the cheese, and Marley— grateful for the hot tea—absent-mindedly began to dunk a custard cream.

The silence was finally broken by Tilly, feeling the need to move things along before Hettie went back to sleep. She grasped the nettle and began. 'What can have happened to bring you out on such a nasty night?' She glanced at Hettie, who was finishing off the boiled ham. 'I'm not sure if it's very late or very early.'

The Butters' bread ovens roared into life. Marley lifted her head and trained her large brown tear-filled eyes first on Tilly, then on Hettie. 'I don't know where to start, but I tink de best place is wid poor Moggy. She told me tings she kept from Miss Marcie, 'cos Miss Marcie, she been so good to her and she didn't want no upset.'

Hettie moved closer to the fire with a knowing nod. 'Yes, we could see how sad Miss Woolcoat was at the death of her . . . er . . . friend. They were very close—that was obvious.'

'Oh my days, Miss Hettie! Not close in dat way! They was sisters, bless you. When Miss Marcie come up wid her winnins and bought Furcross, she gave her sister Alma a job nursin' an' all dat sorta ting, and changed her name to Mogadon so no one would know they was family. You see, dem been estranged for years on account of de mother hatin' Miss Marcie and preferrin' Moggy. Dat mother—she done nasty tings to Miss Marcie, keepin' her locked up, beatin' her, treatin' her real bad, and when little Alma come along a few years later, she turned Miss Marcie out and showered her best love on her new girl kitten. Poor Moggy was torn between her old mother cat and her sister, whom she had come to know and love, but she knew dat if Miss Marcie found out she was still seein' de old mother, she would send her away. So she kept secrets.'

'Which she shared with you?' said Tilly eagerly, getting up to fill the kettle for another round of tea.

Marley wiped a set of large tears from her eyes as she handed her mug to Tilly and continued with her story. 'Moggy—she been sad about her old mother. She told me de old cat was livin' in one of dem hostel places in a bad way, and she had asked Miss Marcie if she could come and live wiv dem at Furcross for her last few years. Miss Marcie got very angry and said Moggy would have to cut de old mother off if she wanted to stay at Furcross and do her nursin', so she pretended to do as her sister say—but all de time she was takin' extra jobs and savin' to get de mother cat a little hut by the sea without tellin' Miss Marcie.'

As fascinating as the life story of Marcia Woolcoat and her sister was, Hettie couldn't help but wonder where all this was leading. The clock on the staff sideboard suggested that it was four o'clock in the morning; the coal bucket was nearly empty, the boiled ham was a memory, and Marley seemed to have settled into a narrative which would fill the *Book at Bedtime* slot for six weeks. Remembering that she was now a detective, she retied her dressing gown cord and sat up a little straighter in her armchair. Just as she was about to take control of the situation, Marley reached into her capacious tote bag and took out a tea caddy; opening it with a flourish, she spread its contents across the rug in front of the fire.

Whatever Hettie had intended to say, the moment was lost, and she and Tilly gasped in unison. Tilly was the first to contribute something more coherent. 'I've never seen so much money in all my life! Is it absolutely real?'

Hettie eyed the bundles of notes as if they were burning a hole in the carpet. She looked across at Marley with renewed interest. 'Oh, Miss Hettie! I know what yer tinkin' but I ain't robbed no bank. It belong to Moggy. She ask me to hide it in me pantry at Furcross till she had enough for de old mother cat's place by the sea, but it's too much money 'ere in me tin. She must have got some big money before she died—so what sorta job pays dis sorta cash? She got 'erself in somethin' bad to do with Miss Pansy and her friends, dat's what I tinkin'—and you and Miss Tilly and de Poppa boy has got to get to de bottom of it.'

Marley subsided into a fresh round of sobbing as Tilly gathered the money up from the rug, placing it in bundles of ten for an easy count up. The total was beyond her wildest dreams and, in spite of Marley's current unhappy state, she found herself daydreaming as to how she might spend it if it were hers. A TV, obviously, a wardrobe full of warm cardigans, a huge packet of crisps that she didn't have to share, enough coal to keep the fire going day and night, an armchair like Hettie's. The list was getting longer and longer, and it was a few moments before she realised that Hettie had been speaking for some time and that Marley Toke had stopped crying to listen.

'It's very clear that Nurse Mogadon took her own life because she felt guilty—the note she left her sister confirms that. But what did she feel guilty *about?* Whatever she did, she was paid a lot of money for it—but why, and by whom? And what made her kill herself in the end?'

'That's easy—someone must have found her out,' Tilly said, poking the fire back to life and adding some of Hettie's business cards to the flames for extra heat. 'Maybe it was blackmail,' she suggested, remembering a similar case fictionalised by Polly Hodge, one of her favourite authors; as she recalled, it had been something to do with a nurse and a funnel. 'We need to go back to the beginning and work out who stole the bodies in the first place, then dumped them at Malkin and Sprinkle. Do you think Alma Mogadon was capable of doing that?' She addressed her question directly to Marley, who sat shaking her head, her large hoop earrings rotating like Catherine wheels.

'No, Miss Tilly, I can't believe she would do such a ting—but you talkin' blackmail give me an idea. Dat day, before she died, she told me de Digger man had sent her a nasty letter.'

'You mean Digger Patch, the gardener?' Hettie interrupted, cramming the banknotes back into Marley's tea caddy.

'Yes. She said he had a racket goin' wid de coffins and she had told him to stop it or she would tell Miss Marcie. He was stealin' de treasures out of de boxes before he put de dirt on, grave robbin' she called it, so he sent her a threatenin' letter and I know she was frightened, but it slipped me mind, what wid her bein' dead.'

In spite of the rain beating down outside, Hettie was suddenly aware of a blue sky moment: if Digger Patch was a grave robber, it was only a very small leap from bits of jewellery to whole bodies. As far as she was concerned, it was

70

definitely case solved this time, and—with very little thought for the vast amount of money nestling in Marley Toke's tea caddy or what Nurse Mogadon might have done to earn it— she roused herself from her armchair, ready to face what she was now sure would be a triumphant day for the No. 2 Feline Detective Agency.

The smell of freshly baked bread filled the cats' nostrils and the Butters' bread ovens warmed their little room, taking the edge off the cold as the fire whimpered and died in the grate. Tilly— still troubled by the tea caddy full of money and Hettie's misplaced euphoria regarding Digger Patch—busied herself in collecting mugs and folding blankets, and Marley was just struggling to her feet when there was a discreet tap at the door. Hettie approached nervously, prepared to receive a verbal termination of their tenancy, but instead a tray of hot sausage rolls and three bacon baps was thrust into her paws. Beryl Butter didn't stay long enough to be thanked, and strode off to help Betty wrestle another batch of tiger loaves from oven number one.

Betty and Beryl Butter were from Lancashire. They believed firmly in a full stomach being the secret to a long and happy life, and had practised this philosophy since they were old enough to roll out pastry on their mother's kitchen table. Bertha Butter had raised her twin girls to delight in the art of food and had educated them in the

71

sheer joy of pies, cakes and pastries, as well as reading them the occasional bedtime story by Catrin Cookpot, a local historical novelist whose take on the poor and needy gave Betty and Beryl a real sense of community spirit. And so it was that—when their mother shuffled off to the great kitchen range in the sky—the Butter twins moved south and invested their small inheritance in what was then a run-down high street bakery. Within weeks they had become royalty, and their bloomers, splits and baps expanded into pies and fancy cakes as their clientele grew in size and physical proportion.

The fact that the Butters had offered Hettie their ground floor storeroom as a bolt hole when her 'shed with a bed' accommodation was reduced to kindling in the great storm was not entirely an act of charity: both Beryl and Betty were very aware of her role in getting their pies into the *Tastes Lovely* range at Malkin and Sprinkle. The story goes that Hettie had popped into the department store's food hall one lunchtime and had purchased a steak and kidney pie, only to discover that the said pie contained neither steak nor kidney but a surfeit of gristle and damp pastry. As she was at the time suffering from an extreme lack of funds, she felt it her duty to complain, and returned the pie to the food counter, pointing out to the assistant cowering behind her bacon slicer that the pie in no way resembled anything that could be described as edible, and that if they needed an example of a proper pie they should look no further than the Butters in the High Street. Listening to the one-sided exchange was Mr Malkin himself, who instructed his assistant, Miss Doris Lean, to remove the pies from sale and offer Hettie anything her heart desired from their cooked meat range. The matter dealt with, he strode off to collect his hat and coat and was later seen devouring several pies in the vicinity of the Butters' shop before putting in a substantial daily order to be sold at Malkin and Sprinkle all year round. This new commercial enterprise had lifted the Butters into the mainstream and, as Doris Lean pointed out to Betty in Lavender Stamp's post office queue a few weeks later, it was all down to one of Hettie Bagshot's tantrums.

If Hettie thought for a moment that the Butters would consider throwing her out on her ear, she was—as she often was—very much mistaken, even with midnight callers and irregular rent payments. Later, when Tilly was taken in under the same roof, she too had been made welcome and was viewed by Beryl and Betty as a stabilising presence in Hettie's somewhat erratic life. The rude awakening at three o'clock in the morning and the subsequent sobbing from the mystery visitor had led the Butters to consider that a sticking plaster for three was required; once the day's baking was underway, a tray was hurriedly

73

prepared in the hope that a hot sausage roll could heal any wound.

Hettie swung round with the gift, narrowly missing Tilly who was once again keeping a low profile in the folds of her dressing gown. 'Stick that kettle on—breakfast has just arrived!' she said, making no effort to contain her excitement.

'Why would they do that?' Tilly asked, as she spread the cloth on Hettie's desk, ready to receive the Butters' treats. 'I thought they were going to throw us out. I started thinking about where we could go and how happy we've been here, but instead they've brought us lovely things. Come on, Marley! Tuck in while I make the tea. There's one bacon and two sausage rolls each.'

'Oh my days! You girls got ya paws under de table 'ere all right! I just take meself a bacon one, as I got to get me back to Furcross in time for breakfast or Miss Marcie will dispense wid me services.' Marley pushed the bacon roll into her mouth, freeing her paws to fasten her coat. She downed the scalding tea that Tilly had made for her and vanished into the early morning rain, promising to catch up with Hettie later in the day.

Alone at last, Hettie and Tilly slumped over their breakfast, exhausted but energised by the night's business and by the added bonus of a plateful of sausage rolls, which Hettie was getting through as if she hadn't eaten for several weeks.

'Maybe we should save a couple for Poppa?'

Tilly suggested as her friend reached out for Marley's share. Hettie thought very carefully, studying the perfection of the sausage roll she had been about to eat; in a rare moment of willpower, she put the object of her affection back on the tray and turned her attention to the mug of tea that was now cool enough to drink. Tilly removed the sausage rolls to a place of safety and wrapped them in a napkin to give to Poppa later, then continued with her own breakfast, setting aside one of her own sausage rolls for any emergency that might occur later in the day.

Satisfied and full, Hettie sat back from the table. After a cursory wipe round her mouth and ears with paws that were still sticky with pastry, she glanced across at her friend, noticing how tired she looked. The last few days had taken their tol , and although Tilly always put a brave face on the constant pain she suffered from her arthritis, Hettie knew that disturbed nights and cold days were not the kindest of situations. 'I think you should stay and run the office today,' she said. I shall go to Furcross when Poppa gets here and have a word with Digger Patch. He has some explaining to do before I wrap things up with Marcia Woolcoat. You could work on our rate sheets ready to quote for the next job, and answer the phone if . . . er . . . I mean *when* it rings.'

Relieved to stay at home, Tilly brightened at the prospect of being an office cat for the day;

with a sausage roll for lunch and as much tea as she could drink thanks to Poppa's generosity, things were looking up—but there were one or two observations she felt she must make before Hettie left for Furcross. 'I think you should have a quick look round Nurse Mogadon's room if Miss Woolcoat will let you,' she began, hoping that Hettie was in one of her responsive moods. 'You might find the letter from Digger Patch that Marley mentioned, and there could be some clues to where all that money came from.'

Hettie was grateful to Tilly, although she did her best not to show it; the day ahead of her was one she would much rather have spent tucked under a blanket in her armchair as the fire crackled in the grate. The promise of winter in these late September days did very little to lift her spirits, and returning to Furcross to take up where she had left off the day before filled her with dread; even the 'as and when' free lunch and tea held no joy after such a fine breakfast. But Marcia Woolcoat owed her money, and Digger Patch needed to be exposed for the unpleasant cat that he was. When the idea of becoming a private detective had struck her during a performance of the long-running play *A Mouse Trapped*, she had never dreamt that she would have to encounter such damaged, difficult and, in some cases, dead members of society. It all seemed so simple in the theatre or on television, which reminded her to procure some batteries for the radio before Sunday, as they were looking forward to the final part of *Cat on a Hot Tinned Roof* with Elizabeth Traybake.

'I think I'm going to have to share all I know with Marcia Woolcoat as soon as I get there,' Hettie sighed, 'but I suppose I should keep the money out of it, at least until we find out what her sister did to get it. It would land Marley in loads of trouble.'

Tilly nodded sagely, then had a thought of her own. 'In proper offices they have lunch breaks. Do you think we should have a lunch break? Because today's Friday and that's library van day outside the Post Office.'

Hettie waited for Tilly to continue with her train of thought, assuming that it might have some bearing on the case, but as nothing further was forthcoming, she addressed the issue of staff lunch breaks. 'I suppose twenty minutes would be allowed under extreme circumstances.'

'Does that include the library van, or perhaps a visit to Jessie's Charity Shop?' asked Tilly, mentally planning her day. 'Because if I don't take my books back, I'll have to pay a fine. And if I don't go to Jessie's, I won't have anything to wear for the fashion show tomorrow night. My best cardigan needs a wash after yesterday, and there isn't anything else in my drawer that will be warm enough. I know Jessie will lend me something that I can take back on Monday.'

Hettie had quite forgotten about the prospect of a night out, and brightened instantly when she realised that she had a treat to look forward to. 'What if we said twenty minutes for lunch and two tea breaks of ten minutes each? Do you think you could manage to fit all your errands in around that framework?'

Tilly—visibly excited at the prospect of a shopping expedition and a chance to choose three new books—agreed to Hettie's generous arrangements, taking into account that if Hettie wasn't in the office, she wouldn't know how long she had been out anyway. Her friend, Jessie, loved a gossip, and you couldn't choose three library books in a hurry; she could easily compensate for the lost time by giving their room a jolly good clean while Hettie was out of the way.

Now that the day's labours had been allocated, the two cats moved about the room, making themselves presentable. Hettie selected what she called her warm business slacks, with a rather over-the-top striped jumper; her best mac looked as if it had been through a war zone, so she completed her Friday look with an old army greatcoat that had seen her through many a cold winter of touring. Tilly pounced on one of her oldest but best-loved cardigans with a hood, ready for her almost all day at home; as the cardigan was several sizes too big for her, it reached the floor and, to keep the draughts out, she pulled on a pair of red woollen socks that should perhaps have been washed several weeks ago.

Before Hettie left for Furcross, she filled the coal scuttle from the coal mountain in the Butters' backyard, another perk they were happy to offer on the understanding that Hettie counted the coal sacks when they were delivered to make sure that the order was correct; there had been some unpleasantness in the past which had resulted in the Butters withdrawing their custom from a local coal merchant who had fiddled them out of two sacks of smokeless.

Tilly waved Hettie off as she clambered into Poppa's van. When he had pulled away, Lavender Stamp bustled out of her post office and positioned herself in the middle of the road, halting the traffic in both directions while she directed the library van into its prime position outside her premises—prime for her rather than for the avid readers, who would never have chosen to venture that far up the High Street. Lavender's Friday takings had boomed since she wrestled the van out of the Methodist Hall car park on the premise that libraries should not be entrenched in any particular denomination, and that her post office was neutral territory. Seeing the mobile library safely parked up, Tilly returned home to sort out her books and get her chores out of the way so that she could concentrate on the nice bits of her day.

CHAPTER FIVE

With the exception of a Marley Toke cooked lunch, there would be no nice bits in Hettie's day. She had resigned herself to a difficult Friday, and even Poppa cautioned her to take care as he swung out of the Furcross car park *en route* to a gas boiler that 'had a mind of its bloody own'. He promised to return as backup in time for the Furcross midday meal, or, if things had gone badly, to give Hettie a lift home.

As Hettie approached the front door, she noticed that the usual collection of observers was missing from the bay window, and it occurred to her that the unexpected death of Nurse Mogadon might have led the mad and bad residents to show some respect by not engaging in their usual daily pursuits. As often happened in Hettie's world, she was wrong—and this became very clear when her polite knock was answered by Marcia Woolcoat, looking every bit the puffed-up, self-important entrepreneur she had projected in their first meeting.

'Miss Bagshot, what a surprise! Is this a social call?' Hettie could do nothing but blink in amazement as Marcia Woolcoat all but dragged her into the entrance hall, divested her of her greatcoat and marched her down the corridor to the parlour, slamming the door behind them. The parlour showed no signs of its former sadness: no body, no tea trolley, and—interestingly—no photographs of Marcia with her now late sister. It was as if the room had been sanitised, with all human frailty put firmly back into a drawer in Marcia Woolcoat's sideboard.

Struggling to adjust to the new situation, Hettie eventually found some words. 'Miss Woolcoat, I must apologise for our hurried departure yesterday, but under the . . . er . . . circumstances, my colleagues and I thought it best to leave you with your grief.' She thought she was doing well, and added. 'I understand that Alma Mogadon was your younger sister and . . .'

Without warning, Marcia Woolcoat sprang at Hettie, forcing her back into an armchair. 'My relationship with her has nothing to do with you!' she hissed. 'There are family matters to deal with, but I won't be needing a detective to solve those.' Regaining her composure, Marcia sat down on the sofa opposite Hettie and, in a softer tone, began a more rational response. 'My sister and I hardly knew each other. I gave her the opportunity to come and work at Furcross because she was a good nurse and shared my ideals regarding the kind and thoughtful ending of lives that had run their course. The fact that she chose to end her own life in such a public and dramatic way, having clearly squandered the trust I invested in her regarding three of my A-list clients, leaves me to deduce that she was entirely unsuitable for the job.'

This was Hettie's make-or-break moment, and she grasped it with both paws. 'I appreciate your disappointment in Nurse Mogadon's behaviour, but some information has come to light regarding a threatening letter sent to her, which may well be the reason she took her own life. She had discovered that one of your residents has been stealing from the coffins in your burial area, and I have reason to believe that her discovery is linked to the missing bodies.' Hettie was pleased with her phrasing, and—in her opinion—she sounded every bit the detective, but Marcia Woolcoat had seen a glimmer of redemption for her sister and waded in.

'What are you trying to say, Miss Bagshot? That my sister . . . I mean, Nurse Mogadon, was innocent? And who is this resident? And what did the letter say?'

There were a number of questions that needed answers but—remembering Poppa's advice to proceed with caution—Hettie decided to keep her cards close to her tabby chest and broach the subject of money before more revelations were shared. 'I need to establish some facts before I'm able to answer your questions. That will require further investigation, which I am prepared to do if you are happy to continue with our financial arrangement. I have been working on the case now for three days and most of last night, and my operatives and I have managed to locate, collect and reinter Misses Vita, Virginia and Pansy to their rightful resting places. Our labours have paid off so far, but any further investigations leading to what I call "nailing the case" will require another payment on account.'

With a barely noticeable nod, Marcia Woolcoat conceded that a further payment was due and stretched out for the biscuit tin that had obligingly paid Hettie's rent earlier in the week. 'Will another three pounds be acceptable? I find myself a little short of ready funds, and would have to visit the bank if you needed more at the moment. I should tell you, though, that I am expecting some definite results for my money.'

Hettie took the notes eagerly and folded them twice to fit into the front pocket of her business slacks. 'Thank you, Miss Woolcoat. I assure you that the case is becoming clearer to me as we speak, but I will need your permission to search your sis . . . er . . . Nurse Mogadon's private room, and, after lunch, I will need to speak with one or two of your residents before reporting my findings to you.' Hettie raised the topic of lunch as the smell of curry flooded her senses and lifted her spirits; a hot meal delivered via Marley Toke's ladle was definitely something to look forward to.

Marcia sat in silent contemplation for a moment or two, then rose from her sofa. 'Follow me, Miss Bagshot. I'll show you to the staff quarters and leave you to your work. Most of the residents are out this morning, as Mr Slack avails us of his minibus on Fridays to enable them to go shopping. They were keen to buy new outfits for the dinner and fashion show at Malkin and Sprinkle tomorrow night, but they'll all be back for lunch so you may speak with them after that. I need to stress that any further disruption to their routine is by no means beneficial to the peaceful life we are able to offer them here at Furcross.'

Hettie felt another mission statement on the way and decided to move things along by opening the door to allow Marcia Woolcoat to sail off down the corridor. The aroma of Marley Toke's dish of the day had become almost unbearable by the time they reached the kitchen block, and they found Marley sitting astride an old milk churn peeling a mountain of sweet potatoes.

'Ah, Marley—I wonder if I could borrow you for a moment? Miss Bagshot wishes to have a look at Nurse Mogadon's room. Would you be kind enough to show her the way and return the key to me when she is finished?' She thrust a key into Marley's paw, turned on her heel and bustled back down the corridor before Marley had a chance to respond.

Wiping her paws on her apron, Marley watched

Marcia's progress until she reached the door to her parlour at the end of the hallway. 'It's a black day for her, Miss Hettie. She don't know how to feel. Her world's come down on her like a ton a mangos from de sky, an' she blamin' Alma for it all. How we gonna fix this?'

Hettie, eyeing up the vat of curry bubbling away happily on the stove, knew that the pressure was on for her to solve the case to the satisfaction of her paying client; if that meant being a little creative with the truth, then so be it. 'I think we have to keep the ageing mother cat story to ourselves for now,' she said, watching with admiration as Marley hauled a batch of freshly made samosas out of the oven. The golden brown triangles glistened as Marley removed them one by one to the warming cabinet by the serving hatch, which was currently closed. Although Tilly hated curry, she was very partial to what she called 'an Indian turnover', and Hettie made a mental note to make sure she took one home for her friend's supper.

'I tink you be right dere, Miss Hettie, but dis money in me tin—dat's worryin' me. It should be Miss Marcie's now Moggy's gone, and de old mother cat should *know* she's gone.' Marley finished her task with the samosas, handing Hettie a sample to try. She gave the curry an aggressive stir before the two cats left the kitchen through the back door and headed out across a small yard, peppered with terracotta pots and boasting large quantities of catnip ripe for harvest. 'Dem's me 'erbs. Dem's magic for me cookin', and me got lots more dryin' in me pantry for de winter.' Hettie spluttered on her very hot samosa at the abundance of not-quite-legal plants which were engulfing the small courtyard, and wondered how Marcia Woolcoat would react to a raid on her premises. Catnip was an indulgence that most enjoyed and very few talked about. It offered a serenity of mind that didn't conform with the hustle and bustle of everyday life, and consequently some-one had decided to ban it. Like most laws, the decision was viewed, talked about and then ignored, and the adult population made up its own mind. Marley Toke, on acquiring the position of Head of Catering at Furcross, had decided to import a particularly happy strain of catnip seed from her homeland; it had been keeping the residents happy for some time, as the herb found its way into most dishes, and those who preferred to be miserable simply avoided any of the dishes prefixed with the word 'Jamaican'.

As Hettie took in the abundance of Marley's kitchen garden, she recalled an incident on one of her summer tours. She had been making her way to the stage across a sea of festivalgoers when she encountered Marley's smoking tent and allowed herself a small pipe before going on to perform her 'blood and thunder' set. Leaving the tent, she noticed that the grass and trees had taken on a rainbow hue; by the time she reached the stage and reunited herself with her band and her twelve-string guitar, her cat's-eye view of life had become almost too colourful. Striking up a medley of Scottish and Irish jigs, played a little faster than usual, she moved on to her current crowd-pleaser—a long and bloody murder ballad in which a noble cat kills his wife and her lover with a broad sword. The song progressed well to the middle of the story, but Hettie's twelve string began to fight back after a rather ambitious sequence of chords that she had made up on the spot; bewildered, the rest of the band continued with the original version and it took some time for Hettie to get back on course. Seeing her distress, Poppa mouthed the first line of the next verse at her from behind one of the monitor wedges in front of the stage, and she eventually brought the song to its bloody conclusion some twenty minutes later, much to the joy and relief of her fans. In the cold light of day, Hettie promised herself never to indulge prior to a performance again and decided to drop that particular piece from future gigs, just to be on the safe side.

Pulling herself back to the present she observed a single-storey, brick-built structure on the other side of the yard. A notice on the door identified it as Furcross Hospital Wing, a rather grand statement considering that the small building also managed to house private bedsitters for the late Nurse Mogadon and the very much alive Marley Toke. Marley pulled open the outer door and led the way past a number of rooms to the bottom of the hallway. Stopping at the final door, she withdrew the key from her apron pocket and hesitated for a moment before unlocking it.

Alma Mogadon lay in her bed, as if she had simply forgotten to get up that day. To see the corpse again so soon shocked Hettie, and she nervously picked samosa crumbs off her striped jumper. Noticing her distress, Marley switched on a table lamp, instantly giving the room a less gloomy appearance. They made a mutual decision to keep the curtains closed—out of respect, and because Hettie had spotted Digger Patch lurking on a bench outside the nurse's window.

'If you needs me to stay, I will,' Marley said, tidying Alma Mogadon's bedclothes around her as if she were tucking her in for the night. 'Me sang her soul to a better place yesterday, so she not 'ere any more. Just what we packaged in, dat's all dere is 'ere in de bed. Miss Marcie, she still decidin' what to do wid de body.'

After the events of the past few days, Hettie couldn't help but think that Alma Mogadon's body was much safer in her own bed than in a casket at the mercy of Digger Patch. Holding that thought, she waved Marley off back to her kitchen and scanned the little room for a place to start her search. In all the detective films she had watched with Tilly, a room search was usually done in quite an aggressive manner, often beginning with the door kicked in to gain entry, then followed by the systematic destruction of furniture, floorboards, mattresses and anything that could be pulled off the walls. Admittedly, the incumbent was usually absent while the search was carried out, and Hettie felt that a velvet paw approach was more appropriate in the presence of the dead nurse, whether her soul had departed via Jamaican Airways or not.

Starting with the bedside table, she gently worked her way through Alma Mogadon's life. Mercifully, the nurse had not been a hoarder of unnecessary things, but there were personal treasures that—now she was no longer alive— seemed meaningless to an outsider: a pebble from a beach; a conker from an autumn; a small linen bag of brightly coloured marbles; a sketchbook which testified to happy days doodling in the sun. Hettie's mind wandered again into her own past, stored away in a somewhat haphazard fashion in the small shed by the Butters' vegetable plot: her neglected guitar; boxes of her albums; posters and photographs of a life that seemed to belong to someone else. If she no longer valued her achievements, what would happen to them all when she was gone? Hettie began to understand a little better why Marcia Woolcoat buried her residents with their prized possessions; better that way than bundled into a dustbin bag and buried in a forgotten hole in the earth. It made Digger Patch's grave thefts even more despicable—no doubt he cast off anything of real sentimental value before selling the good stuff. Hettie found herself almost looking forward to her interview with the deposed celebrity gardener.

She had left looking under the bed until last, mainly because of the body lying on it. The room had become almost tomb-like as she worked her way round it and she had, in her imagination, convinced herself that the bed held secrets that only she was destined to discover—if she could be brave enough to go there. She was not disappointed. Lifting the bedspread and folding it back across Alma Mogadon's body, Hettie lay on the floor and reached under the bed for a shoebox covered in dust. Even to her untrained eye, it had not been opened for some time. Then came the box file, which interested her more as it had recently been dragged through the dust under the bed, its contents obviously viewed or added to within the last few weeks. Opening the file, her attention was instantly drawn to a letter, addressed by hand and kept in place by the spring inside the box. There had been no real attempt to hide it, and it was clearly the most recent addition to a number of similar letters written in the same paw. Not wishing to linger any longer than she had to with her very silent companion, Hettie put the boxes on the table by the lamp and opened the letter that had caught her attention.

It was from Digger Patch, short and very much to the point:

I KNOW THE CASKETS WERE EMPTY AND THAT YOU TOOK THE BODIES. EITHER YOU PAY UP OR YOUR NASTY LITTLE SECRET IS OUT. KEEP YOUR MOUTH SHUT IF YOU KNOW WHAT'S GOOD FOR YOU. D.P.

Putting the letter to one side, Hettie opened some of the others. It soon became clear that Digger Patch was very much aware of Alma Mogadon's family problems and had used the information to extract payments as silence money. Some of the letters mentioned other Furcross residents, and hinted at a number of 'difficulties' that had beset them in their earlier lives; and there were personal obscenities aimed at Alma, who, in the past, had clearly fought off Patch's advances—something which Hettie was convinced lay at the root of his vindictive behaviour. It didn't really change the fact that Alma Mogadon had been involved in the removal of the bodies, and according to Marley Toke's tea caddy, she had been paid handsomely for it. If Digger Patch hadn't stumbled across

91

the empty caskets, Alma would still be alive and her mother would be moving to the seaside. But who had Nurse Mogadon sold the bodies to, and why? It was impossible to be certain about anything, except that Digger Patch was a blackmailer and a petty thief.

Hettie gathered up the bundle of letters and slipped them into an empty folder, then lifted the lid on the dusty shoebox. Very quickly, she realised that it should be removed from prying eyes, as it contained photos of a childhood spent with an adoring mother cat. There were long letters, birthday cards and thank you notes, all in the same paw and all addressed to Lavender Stamp's post office in the High Street, marked for collection only. For fear of losing her sister, Alma Mogadon had hidden her mother's love away in a shoebox, and Hettie decided to remove the deception before it could bring further grief for Marcia Woolcoat. Picking up the box and balancing the blackmail notes on top, she left Alma Mogadon in peace, locking the door behind her before making her way back to the main building just as the lunch bell sounded.

CHAPTER SIX

Tilly had also had a busy morning, cleaning and tidying. It was her intention to have the room spick and span by lunchtime, so that she could do the library van justice before setting out down the High Street to Jessie's charity shop. There was one difficult moment with Hettie's best mac, which Tilly had attempted to sponge down, scrubbing away hard at the piccalilli stains deposited the day before by Marley Toke's ladle; in spite of—or probably because of—her labours, the stain appeared to spread across the mac like an incoming tide. Throwing caution to the wind, Tilly decided to immerse the whole garment in a tin bath full of soap suds in the backyard. She climbed in herself to tread the mac and its stain into submission, and finally achieved a good result, which swung proudly around on the washing line as if showing off to anyone who was interested. Keeping the mac company was an assortment of woolly socks, including the ones Tilly had selected for herself earlier that morning and had quite forgotten to take off before climbing into the bath.

The Butters' pie of the week promotion had been going very well, and Tilly made sure of Friday's supper by exchanging their luncheon vouchers the second that Beryl Butter threw the bolts back on the shop door. She was torn between the steak and kidney—Hettie's favourite—and a sausage and onion recipe, for which the Butters had received a gold medal at the Southwool Pie and Produce Show. Eventually she decided on one of each and two large cream horns for pudding, and was satisfied that whatever sort of day Hettie was having, she would have a feast to come home to.

Placing supper under a tea towel on the staff sideboard, Tilly went about the rest of her chores and wrestled her typewriter out from under Hettie's desk, ready to have a go at the agency's rate sheet later. She had been eyeing up her sausage roll for some time and, seeing that it was nearly twelve, she indulged herself with a cup of tea and a sit down while she tucked into her breakfast leftovers. Then she gathered up her books, skipped out into the High Street, and climbed the steps to Turner Page's library van.

Turner Page had been chief librarian for more years than anyone could remember. Before the old library closed, he had become quite a celebrity, running a number of aggressive campaigns to keep the doors open. But eventually his appetite for chaining himself to the table leg dwindled; when he was the only cat left in the building, with no one to notice his protest, he joined his despondent readers and went home. The library doors closed for the last time, and the bulldozers moved in to make way for a car park and bowling alley.

Before she met Hettie, the old library was Tilly's salvation, especially on cold winter days. The reading room boasted a number of comfortable armchairs, and the big old iron radiators brought warmth and drying facilities to hats, mittens and raincoats as their occupants parked themselves out of the winter chill for a few hours each day. Tilly had had her own library ritual: newspapers in the morning, read on a table that sprawled the length of the room, and then a visit to detective or romantic fiction for something to curl up with until the library bell clanged at six, telling all readers to make their way home. In Tilly's case, home was an old garden shed with a broken window and no door, and there had been times— in the middle of a winter's night—when the cruelness of the frost and snow had kept her awake, frozen to the old shelf she'd adopted as her bed. Only the thought of the library's warmth had kept her alive.

The building had closed at the height of summer, and the true impact of its demise had not been felt until the autumn, when the nights drew in and the first frosts began to bite. That was the winter that Tilly met Hettie, and the two cats found a friendship based on looking out for each other; when Tilly was invited to share

Hettie's small room at the Butters', it had given her life meaning and—most of all—hope. A number of her library acquaintances had perished in the cold that winter. There had been an outcry against those responsible, especially when the bowling alley failed to capture the imagination of the townsfolk and closed within a year, leaving a derelict building inhabited by homeless cats, with plenty of parking spaces and no cars to put in them. The strength of feeling had resulted in a lot of press coverage, and media giants like Hacky Redtop had vowed to put a library back where it belonged at the heart of the community. A great deal of money was raised by local shop-keepers, and some well-known authors—keen to hang onto their royalties—lent their names to the cause.

Turner Page took great pride in his mobile library. Although well into his seventies and much greyer than he used to be, his love of the written word and of those who read spurred him on to polish his bookshelves until they gleamed. The lettering for his categories was bold and delivered with the flourish of an artist, and he was no stranger to innovation: recently, he had made tentative steps into the world of video movies, introducing a small selection for those who could afford the equipment to play them on. Such was his devotion to work that his personal appearance lacked a little attention: most days, he appeared still wearing his pyjamas, covered by a woolly tank top for decency's sake.

Clutching her returns, Tilly made for detective fiction and scanned the shelf for the *H*'s until she found what she was looking for: the latest novel by Polly Hodge, an author she greatly admired. The new book, *An Unsuitable Job for a Cat*, boasted a rather lurid cover of a cat's paw holding a dagger dripping with blood, and Tilly pounced on it with a cry of delight. The queue to have books stamped had died down a little, so she decided to unburden herself of the pile she was returning. Turner Page, who was usually either reading a book or stamping one and very rarely looked up, checked the dates on Tilly's returns and placed them in a box under his desk. Needing to know something, she tried to catch his attention, but a tut from behind forced her back to the shelves and a rather unpleasant-looking male cat slammed his books down to be stamped. As he banged into Tilly on his way out, she noticed that he had selected a number of books on self-improvement; the irony had not gone unnoticed by Turner Page, who looked up, shrugged his bony shoulders and smiled with the twinkliest eyes that Tilly had ever seen. She seized her moment. 'Mr Page, I wonder if you could explain to me what these vid-e-os do? They look like books but I can see they're not, and when I open them there's nothing inside. Your shelf is fuller every time I come to the library van, and I notice that this one has a picture of my favourite actress, Elizabeth Traybake, on the front.'

Turner Page did a rare thing, and came out from behind his counter to assist Tilly in her enquiries. 'My dear Miss . . . er . . . ?'

'Tilly. You can call me Tilly.'

'My dear Miss Tilly, the video is the very latest technology. It enables one to enjoy the delights of cinematography in one's own home at a time of one's own choosing. It is like a book with moving pictures and sound that you can put down or pick up whenever you wish, without the constraints of a television schedule. It is, quite simply, a cinema in one's front room.'

Tilly stared in absolute wonderment at the plastic box that Turner Page had placed in her paws. She turned it round, trying to work out the magic, opening the catch and snapping it shut again as if frightened that something would escape. 'Does it need batteries to make it work?'

'No, my dear, and the box is empty because I have had to impose certain levels of security to guard against theft. Videos are very much the "must-haves" of modern living.' Turner Page returned to his desk and reached behind his chair, pulling out another plastic box slightly smaller than the one glued to Tilly's paws. 'This, my dear, is the actual video. You are holding the box it fits into. Think of it like a dust jacket.'

Tilly was finding it hard to keep up, and tried desperately to remember if there had been any talk of a drink or drug dependency issue regarding Turner Page during her days at the old library. In a last effort to get to the bottom of this seemingly new phenomenon, she took the proffered item and noticed that it rattled and had two plastic spools; it appeared to be a larger version of some of Hettie's old cassette tapes, the ones that Poppa's van chewed up on long journeys. 'If it doesn't need batteries, how does it go and where do the pictures come from?' Tilly began to feel hot tears of frustration well up in her eyes. It was the same whenever she encountered a new gadget. Her favourite, of course, was the television, and she'd been heartbroken on the day that reduced circumstances forced the cat from the rental shop to take the set away—but there had also been much excitement when Hettie turned up with an electric kettle that turned itself off. Tilly had spent days watching it in case it forgot, and it had cost a fortune in coins for their greedy meter. But this video thing—did she need one? Would it help to ease the pain of not having a TV?

Seeing her distress, Turner Page gently removed the video and its case from her paws. 'I feel I have not given you a full and comprehensive introduction to the video,' he said. 'I have offered its joys without the practicalities. It runs on mains electricity. You will need to hire or purchase a video machine which is compatible with your television set, and you will need to tune an empty channel to converse with the video player— which will also be able to record a television programme of your choice if you are out, as long as you have some blank videos.'

Tilly was now more distressed than ever. The thought of leaving a machine in her room that randomly recorded anything it felt like from her television whilst she was out was more than she could bear; life was difficult enough as it was without machines watching TV when she couldn't. Snatching up the latest Polly Hodge, which she'd abandoned earlier, she quickly selected a Nicolette Upstart and an Alexander McPaw Spit to add to her pile; with the books firmly stamped, she fled the library van, looking back over her shoulder in case the videos were chasing her.

CHAPTER SEVEN

The lunchtime rush had been quite spectacular at Furcross. Marley Toke's Jamaican curry was the hit of the week, and the residents—fresh from a morning of retail therapy—positively galloped towards her serving hatch, carrying away plates and trays piled high and returning for large helpings of mango suet pudding drowned in Jamaican custard. Poppa joined Hettie in the queue, having dealt with his unruly boiler, and the pair ate their lunch at a table away from the general scrum so that Hettie could bring him up to speed with her search of Nurse Mogadon's room. Digger Patch had also isolated himself from his fellow inmates, Hettie noticed; he had not gone shopping with them, and now sat at a table for one, picking at what appeared to be a cauliflower cheese—the non-Jamaican option.

'He looks like a cat in a bit of bother,' said Poppa, parcelling up a samosa for later.

Hettie followed suit, remembering that Tilly had missed out on a staff lunch. 'I think we have enough proof to tackle him about the blackmail letters. We could even mention stealing from the caskets, but I doubt he knows much about the bodies going missing so we're back to where we started,' she said despondently, stirring the mango suet into her custard. The night's events had caught up with her, and Marley's excellent lunch made her long for an armchair by a sunny window to catch up on some sleep, but the job was far from done: Digger Patch was responsible for Nurse Mogadon's suicide, and needed to be prevented from spreading his poisonous allegations any further. With that in mind, she rallied slightly, spooned down the rest of her pudding, and loaded up the tray with empty plates for Poppa to return to Marley Toke's hatch.

As Poppa progressed across the dining room, Digger Patch rose from his solitary table and headed towards the French windows and out into the garden. Signalling to her friend, Hettie followed the celebrity gardener at what she considered to be a safe distance, waiting for Poppa to emerge from the dining room and take up a nonchalant but observant position in the shrubbery. Patch strode across the lawn and through to the vegetable garden, where—overlooked by Nurse Mogadon's window—he slumped down on a bench and stared at his gardener's boots.

'Would you mind if I joined you?' Hettie asked. 'It's such a lovely afternoon, and everything looks so fresh in the sun after all that rain last night.'

'Suit yerself. I'm not stoppin' long. I got some potatoes to lift and the last of me salad crops before the frost gets 'em.'

Hettie sensed that Digger Patch was not looking

for company or niceties about the weather, so she decided to cut to the quick, certain that Poppa was ready to spring to her defence if things got nasty. 'Mr Patch,' she began, 'I'm sure you must know that my colleagues and I have been brought in by Miss Woolcoat to investigate the disappearance of three bodies earlier this week from the burial ground at Furcross.'

'Yeah, well, you got that bit wrong straight away,' said Patch, sneering at Hettie's opening gambit. 'Them bodies never reached their graves. They was taken before. The caskets were empty when I came to bury 'em, so before you start accusin' me, I had nothin' to do with it. If you'll excuse me, I have work to do.'

Digger Patch began to rise from the bench but Hettie caught his arm, forcing him down again and surprising herself with her determination to have her say. 'I am aware of that, Mr Patch, and I'm not accusing you of stealing bodies—but it *has* come to light that you are involved in other unpleasant schemes that concern me. It's not just bodies that have been stolen from the coffins. I understand that you have been helping yourself to personal effects belonging to the deceased, and this must be so—you wouldn't know that the bodies were missing if you hadn't tampered with the coffins.'

Digger Patch rounded on Hettie, showing a face that had never been seen by his adoring TV fans.

'If you knows what's good for you, you'll push off and leave me in peace. I can make things difficult for you. I got friends who can make sure you never work again, and they aren't known for bein' nice, if you know what I mean. You obviously have no idea who you are talkin' to, and Miss Woolcoat won't be too pleased when I tell her you been botherin' me.'

Aware that Poppa was only a matter of yards away and in earshot of Patch's threats, Hettie faced the gardener with what she hoped was her best steely stare, then waited a moment for full dramatic effect before turning the screw a little tighter. 'Please feel free to complain to Miss Woolcoat, but don't forget to tell her that you were the reason her sister killed herself and that your nasty letters—sent to Nurse Mogadon—also mentioned other Furcross residents whom Marcia Woolcoat had protected from the outside world. Oh, and that closer to home you had discovered the relationship between Nurse Mogadon and her elderly mother, which she had been keeping from her sister for fear of losing her job. In fact, shall we both go and find Miss Woolcoat now and get this all out in the open? I have your letters, and I would be happy to pass them to Miss Woolcoat for her thoughts on the subject.' Hettie paused. 'Or you could just tell me what happened on the day of the burial.'

She wished that Tilly had been there to witness

her finest moment. Digger Patch toppled from his self-made pedestal and cowered on the bench as if he had been set about with his own garden spade. 'All right, all right—I'll tell you what I know but I don't have long. I've got a train to catch at four. My daughter's expectin' me, see; she wants me to stay with her for a bit.'

The fact that Digger Patch now had a train to catch was no surprise to Hettie, and she had every reason to believe that it would be a one-way ticket. 'Let's go back to Monday,' she said, knowing that vital clues would be lost if she did not ask the right questions regarding the missing bodies. 'What exactly was your part in the burial situation?'

'Same as it always is,' responded the crushed celebrity gardener. 'Nurse Mogadon did her . . . er . . . business in the morning, putting 'em away and tarting 'em up with the cat that does the nails, then she calls for me to help her lift 'em into their caskets and we wheeled 'em across the yard into the dining room with the lids off for the final goodbyes. Then I helps her get 'em back to the hospital wing and leaves her to put the extra bits and pieces into the caskets. She puts the lids on and screws 'em down ready for me to come and collect 'em for the burial. Then I got 'em lined up by the graves. I rings a bell and they all comes across from the main buildin' for some songs and poems before goin' back in for the funeral teas. I stays to bury 'em normally, but I found out there was nothin' to bury so I helped meself to a few trinkets and stuck the caskets behind me potting shed. I was going to fill the graves in, but I twisted me back while I was draggin' one of the boxes and it was comin' on to rain so I knew no one would come out again—it was getting too late and too cold. I meant to fill in the holes the next mornin', but when I woke up me back was so bad I couldn't get out of bed. Then I heard that Nola Ledge had discovered the empty graves and all hell had broken loose, so I lay low and pretended I knew nothing. I went to the hospital wing later to get some help for me back pain, and I saw Nurse Mogadon countin' a big pile of money through the window of the dispensary. As she'd threatened to tell Miss Woolcoat about me takin' stuff from the coffins, I decided to send one of me notes to her about the missin' bodies. Next thing I know, you turn up with the bodies and this mornin' at breakfast Miss Woolcoat announces that the nurse has killed herself and the hospital wing has been closed until further notice.'

Hettie had avoided interrupting Digger Patch's rambling dialogue of events for fear of missing something, and by the end of his story she could easily understand why his publishers were not happy with his work: the word 'soulless' popped into her head, and for a gardener that seemed

106

strange. 'Between dropping the bodies off in the hospital wing and collecting them for burial, did you notice anyone else around besides Nurse Mogadon?'

Digger Patch put his head on one side to think, trying now to be extra helpful. Scratching his chin, he said: 'I seem to think there was one or two visitors that day, but I can't say for sure what time I seen them. Nutty Slack was here, visitin' Nola as usual—I seen him parkin' up his minibus out front and that must have been just before lunch. He didn't stay long—I heard him drivin' off as I brought one of the caskets through to the burial ground. Then there was Marilyn's girl, Cocoa— stuck-up little minx. She's started hangin' out with that Oralia Claw and they're always up here— bloody nuisance, both of 'em, if you ask me: thick as thieves and twice as stupid. They were big friends with Pansy Merlot—brought drink in for her after she'd bin told not to do it any more. Miss Woolcoat had to put a stop to that, but it was too late for Pansy by then. There was a couple of odd jobbers doin' some work on the gutterin' of the hospital wing; they seemed to come an' go as they pleased, but I'm not sure they were here on Monday. Rough pair of low lifes, always seemed to be in their van readin' newspapers, so not much work done there. Oh yes, and I nearly forgot—Miss Woolcoat had a delivery from Malkin and Sprinkle. That was on Monday, after lunch; they had trouble gettin' their big van through the gates and Silas had to help direct 'em in.'

It occurred to Hettie that Monday had been an extremely busy day of comings and goings, and Digger Patch had presented her with a number of possibilities as to how the bodies might have been removed from Furcross. She was beginning to feel exhausted, and she longed for her armchair by the fire and Tilly's constant chatter, but she knew that she would have to speak to Marcia Woolcoat before the end of her day: Miss Woolcoat was expecting results for her money. Realising that her interest in him had begun to wane, Patch rose from the bench and this time Hettie let him go. She watched as he made his way slowly back to the main building, with no further thoughts of lifting his potatoes or saving his salad crops from the frost. At least there would be no more of his 'little notes' to disturb the long-dead secrets of those who had put their trust in Furcross, but that was no consolation for Alma Mogadon, who lay dead only a matter of yards from where Hettie sat.

'Blimey!' said Poppa, emerging from the shrubbery. 'You did well to get all that out of him. You were looking like a proper detective for a minute or two. I expect he's packing his kit and clearing out before you can get back to Marcia Whatsit. Stupid, really—I reckon he was onto a good thing here. If he really has got a daughter, I bet she'll be bracing herself. He's not the sort to muck in, is he?'

'No,' agreed Hettie. 'Alma Mogadon is now firmly in the frame for selling bodies, but in spite of having a clearer view of what happened on Monday, we still have a list of suspects for her accomplice and no real favourite. Was it Nutty Slack the chimney sweep, with or without the help of his friend, Nola Ledge, the retired school-teacher? Or could it be Oralia Claw? I've never liked her since she set up in the High Street. Then there's Cocoa Repel: could she be calling the shots, whilst hiding behind her mother's money? And what about the delivery van from Malkin and Sprinkle? That was where the bodies were dumped, so maybe Lotus Ping was in the back, loading the corpses in while the delivery men were being dominated by Miss Woolcoat.'

Poppa resisted voicing the thought that had just entered his head; it involved black leather and whips, and Hettie caught the boyish twinkle in his eye. The two cats exploded into peals of laughter as the afternoon tea bell clanged in the distance and they made their way across the lawn. Hettie turned to look back, compelled to rest her gaze on the window of Nurse Mogadon's room, and for a very brief moment she fancied she had seen a small, pale face looking at her from behind the glass.

CHAPTER EIGHT

Tilly had not meant to fall asleep when she got back from the library van. All would have gone according to plan if she hadn't treated herself to five minutes in Hettie's armchair to drink her tea and eat the custard cream she had found at the back of the staff sideboard during her morning clean-up. An hour later, she awoke in a panic as several black plastic video boxes surrounded her and threatened to take her television away. Relieved that it had only been a nasty dream, but upset that she had no television to lose, Tilly got up and checked that the pies were still under the tea towel. Remembering Hettie's best mac, she fetched it in from the line along with the socks, pleased that the laundry was almost dry. She eyed the mac up, having felt the chill of the backyard, then slipped it on, expecting it to be several sizes too big for her. To her delight it fitted perfectly, but it was still slightly damp, and it occurred to her that the best way to finish drying it was to wear it herself; by the time she got home from seeing Jessie, her own body heat would have finished the job. Apart from anything else, she felt very important in it, and Hettie need never know.

Pulling on clean red socks and adding a bright

green knitted scarf to the borrowed mac, Tilly made her way out into the High Street, waving to the Butters who were wedged in their shop window, removing the final crumbs of the lunchtime assault on their breads, pies and pastries. Oralia Claw's van was taking up most of the pavement outside her nail bar and, as Tilly passed, Oralia staggered out of her shop under the weight of yet more boxes to be loaded inside. Tilly couldn't quite remember why she didn't like Oralia Claw, but decided that it must be because there was nothing about her *to* like; Hettie didn't like her either, so the negative feelings were built on sound judgement. And besides, the nail bar seemed to attract a certain sort of silly female cat—painted, pinched and pretending to be posh, the sort that would wobble their stiletto heels through fire to attract the overpaid brawn of the local football team with their fast cars and low intellect.

Oralia Claw's place in the community had engaged Tilly's thoughts in such an entertaining way that she almost missed the turning into Cheapcuts Lane, where her friend Jessie ran a charity shop from her front room. Exactly *which* charity had never been explained, but the outlet had become so well established that no one asked any more; the old adage of such things beginning at home seemed to fit Jessie's philosophy of life, and she provided the less well-off in town with an Aladdin's cave of clothes and bric-a-brac, as well as a popular channel for the better-heeled to get rid of unwanted good stuff. Strangely enough, it was the better-heeled who made the shop a success, as they also bought from its 'posh but not quite new range'—a rail of clothing that was pushed into the centre of the shop whenever Jessie saw a decent car pull up outside.

Tilly loved looking in the charity shop window: her friend prided herself on her window displays—always seasonal and colour-coordinated to catch the eye of any cat who had deviated from the High Street. Today, Jessie had gone for an 'autumn in the rain' look, with umbrellas, wellington boots and a rather fine mannequin posed in a bright yellow storm cape with matching sou'wester. The effect was enhanced by a scattering of leaves, some assorted nuts and a stuffed squirrel, and Tilly purred with appreciation. She went inside, her arrival announced by a peal of bells which dangled on strings across the door.

Jessie sat behind a large kitchen table which doubled as shop counter. A cloche hat of red velvet was perched on her head, and her matching red and purple shawl seemed to have become a little too involved with the garment she was knitting. A pair of red-rimmed spectacles made its bid for freedom when she spotted Tilly, and was only saved from disaster by a cord that tethered it round a long-haired tabby neck. 'Well, there's a sight for sore eyes,' Jessie said, abandoning her knitting to give Tilly a hug. 'I was only thinking about you this morning. An old dear came in and offered me some really nice cardigans—lovely bright colours with easy buttons, right up your street! And wait for it—some of them had pockets and hoods! I bought them up for a song. In fact, I'm thinking of turning my whole window display over to knits next week. Why don't you have a look through them while I stick the kettle on? It's high time we had a catch-up, and I think there's a chocolate biscuit with your name on it in the tin.' Jessie slid a box across the floor and Tilly clapped in sheer delight at the rainbow of woollen cardigans, all flailing their arms to escape their incarceration. Picking and prodding at them, she selected the three that she was most taken by and divested herself of Hettie's mac, unbuttoning her old, well-loved cardigan ready to try the new ones.

'Oh, come into the back to do that,' said Jessie, heading for the shop door. 'I'll shut up for a bit while we have some tea.' She turned the 'back in a tick' sign to face any hopeful customers and shot the bolt across, then picked up the box of cardigans and led Tilly—still clutching her favoured three—through to her private quarters.

Jessie's back room had been her home for as long as she could remember. She had been taken in by a kind elderly cat when she was five weeks old, after being abandoned—along with her dead mother—at the gates of a hostel, tied up in a rubbish bag. Miss Lambert—a keen supporter of the hostel—had adopted Jessie and raised her as her own, leaving her small terraced house to her when she died. Jessie had loved Miss Lambert. For an elderly cat, she was a great deal of fun to be with and had taught Jessie the ways of the world, encouraging her in the appreciation of beautiful things—especially if they happened to be red. Jessie had nursed Miss Lambert in her final years and, when their money ran out, had enterprisingly turned their front room into a shop of all sorts. Although money was still often scarce, Jessie had hung on to her legacy, taking extra jobs here and there when the shop was going through one of its quiet periods. Tilly, too, had much to thank Miss Lambert for: they had met at the old library and—seeing that Tilly was in great need of a decent dinner—the older cat had brought her home one cold October day. From that moment on, Tilly and Jessie had been firm friends; in fact, it was Jessie who had first encouraged Tilly's passion for cardigans, and the rest—as they say—is history.

The room was swathed in red, with a Turkish carpet on the floor and a slightly beaten-up sofa, which displayed two rich-red carpet cushions and a soft chenille throw; the lampshades were hung with red tassels, and the scent of sandalwood and jasmine drifted from incense sticks by the fireplace. Tilly loved this room; it had hardly changed since Miss Lambert died and—looking now at her friend, pouring tea from a red pot—she realised for the first time that Jessie was indeed becoming Miss Lambert, a vision straight from the Marrakesh Express.

'Come on, then—tell me your news,' said Jessie, sinking into one of the large cushions on the sofa and patting the space beside her for Tilly to sit down. 'How's Hettie getting on with her new career? Any takers in the world of gumshoes and private eyes?'

Tilly dragged herself away from the cardigans and accepted a cup of what she called 'perfumed tea', guessing that Earl Grey must have always served his hot drinks with a chocolate biscuit, if only to take the taste away. 'Well, it was a bit slow to start with. We almost gave up,' she spluttered through a mouthful of crumbs. 'Then the phone rang on Wednesday with a proper case and Hettie's been on it ever since. She even let me help yesterday. There were bodies everywhere! We had to collect them from Malkin and Sprinkle 'cos someone had dug them up, and the gardener's been stealing things out of the coffins, and the nurse killed herself in front of the TV. We had to move her on a tea trolley.'

Throughout Tilly's brief but thorough appraisal

of the case, Jessie sat with her eyes wide and her mouth even wider in a silent scream of amazement. When Tilly paused for a moment to take another bite of her biscuit, she felt obliged to challenge the credibility of the story. 'What? Bodies, gardeners, coffins, suicides and tea trolleys? Sounds like a bad crime fiction series. You are joking, aren't you?' Watching Tilly's face and waiting for the burst of laughter that never came, she realised that her friend was serious. 'Oh my God! Where did all this happen?'

Feeling very important, as the bearer of revelations always does, Tilly fleshed out her macabre bullet points, much to Jessie's delight. By the time she had finished, Jessie's tea was cold and her biscuit untouched, and Jessie was ready to sign up as a recruit to the No. 2 Feline Detective Agency—as a plant, or as anything else that would allow her to share in the excitement. 'Wow!' she said. 'Fancy Furcross being involved in all this! Marcia gets a lot of her designer stuff from me—always buys a size too small and takes all the lemon, beige and pink stuff, which is fab 'cos no one else would be seen d . . . er . . . out in it. Marilyn Repel swaps a lot of her more stagey stuff for everyday wear with me, too, and I know Cocoa quite well—she offers me work occasionally at her shows, dressing the models backstage. I'm helping her tomorrow night at Malkin and Sprinkle. But I'll never understand why she's taken up with that Claw creature—no talent, no brain, no dress sense, just hitching a ride on Cocoa's fame and Marilyn's fortune. She's a nasty, thin piece of work if you ask me, but I think the show will be good. Cocoa has put a lot of work into her designs.'

'Oh good!' said Tilly, scrambling off the sofa and selecting the first cardigan to try. 'We're going to that. We got free tickets from Mr Sprinkle when we picked the bodies up. What about this one? It's lovely and warm, but the sleeves are a bit long. The pockets and the hood are really nice, though, and it's got lots of purple in it.'

Jessie admired Tilly's choice. 'The colour really suits you and you can always roll the sleeves up a bit. Try the red one—that's got a zip and you could wear it over another cardigan to go out in.'

Tilly was having a lovely time, and soon discovered that all three cardigans had become firm favourites. The final one—in blue with bright yellow and red buttons—made her look years younger, and she decided that it would be perfect for the fashion event; it even had a small silver fleck running through the wool, which made it the perfect choice for evening wear. But, as often happens when a good time is being had, reality struck the cruellest of blows.

'I'm not sure any of them are quite right for me,' she said reluctantly. 'I think I'll leave it for today. I should be going—Hettie will be back soon and I promised to do some typing for her.'

Jessie watched as Tilly carefully folded the cardigans and put them back in the box, remembering what Miss Lambert had said about her: 'That cat will always want for something because she's too proud to ask.' Knowing that dignity and self-respect were priceless commodities, Jessie leant forward to help Tilly as she struggled back into her old cardigan. 'I've got a bit of a problem tomorrow,' she said. 'I'm supposed to be at Malkin and Sprinkle by lunchtime, which means I'll have to shut the shop for the afternoon, and Saturday is my busiest day. I don't suppose you could look after things for me, could you? Most of the stuff is priced and the rest you can take offers on. I haven't got any cash but I can pay you in cardigans if Hettie could spare you for the afternoon?'

Tilly beamed, skipped and finally jumped into the box of cardigans, retrieving the blue, purple and red objects of her desire. Jessie smiled in a satisfied sort of way and gave a nod to Miss Lambert, whose ashes took centre stage on the mantelpiece in a beautiful red and gold Chinese urn. 'That settles it then,' said Jessie, rising from her sofa. 'I'd better open up again for a couple of hours. I might catch the Methodists coming out of their Friday whisker drive. God knows what they do in that hall all afternoon, but it certainly puts them in the mood for my bric-a-brac section on their way home. Since that bloody woman from the post office had the library van moved up her end, trade has dropped off a bit for me on Fridays, so I'll grab anything I can—even the Methodists!'

Tilly chuckled as she followed Jessie through to the shop, barely able to see over the three cardigans she was carrying. Jessie found a suitable bag while Tilly made herself at home once again in Hettie's mac, hastily abandoned in the excitement of the new knits. 'What time would you like me tomorrow? I'd rather be here early so you can show me the ropes. I've never worked for cardigans before, so I'll need to do a good job for you.'

'Come about twelve—we'll have an hour to go through everything. I'll make us a sandwich, so don't bother with lunch—and I'm dying to find out how Hettie got on at Furcross. That's worth three cardigans of anyone's money.' The two cats laughed. Bidding farewell to her new recruit, Jessie returned to her knitting and braced herself for the Methodists, while Tilly skipped all the way home with her three new best cardigans.

CHAPTER NINE

Tea at Furcross was an unusually quiet affair for a Friday. Only a handful of residents had bothered to leave their rooms to partake of Marley Toke's lemon drizzle triple-layer cake; most were busy squeezing themselves into their chosen finery as a trial run for Saturday's night out, and an extra slice of cake could be the difference between a cocktail dress fitting or not. The situation didn't seem to deter Marcia Woolcoat: as Hettie and Poppa stepped through the French windows, she was positioning the largest slice of cake on her plate—perhaps to compensate for the others' lack of interest, but probably because she was just plain greedy. Marcia nodded to Hettie, collected a cup of tea from Marley Toke's serving hatch, and disappeared back down the corridor to her parlour.

'Not exactly in mourning for her sister, is she?' noted Poppa, attacking the drizzle cake with enthusiasm. 'Do you think she should be on our list of suspects?'

Hettie stirred her tea thoughtfully. 'Well, she's a bit strange, but I can't see her bringing all this trouble on herself and I think her heart's in the right place. She didn't have to set this place up with her windfall. She could have lived an easy life wherever she chose, and let's face it—all this business isn't going to do her much good. A lot of her guests have left already, she now has no nurse to keep them going or help them on their way out, and by the end of today the gardener will have cleared off. I'm not surprised she needs a big piece of cake.'

Poppa agreed as Marley emerged from her hatch and made her way over to their table. 'Miss Hettie—what shall I do wid dat shoebox from Moggy's room? I know I said I'd keep it safe for you, but Miss Marcie, she just been askin' me if you found anythin' in her room when you done the searchin', and she asked if there was any letters or anythin' like dat. I tink she knows me's coverin' up for Moggy, and I worryin' meself sick about dat money in me tin. If she finds out I bin keepin' tings from her, she'll turn me out and den where will I be? Oh my days! Miss Hettie, I been so happy here with me cookin' and me nice room and a place to grow me magic plants.'

Marley was working herself up into a highly emotional state, and with every good reason; Hettie knew she would have to choose her words very carefully in her final interview of the day if she was to protect her friend. She looked across at Poppa for inspiration, and he didn't disappoint: wiping the icing sugar from his whiskers, he stood up and attempted to put his arm round the sizeable shoulders of Marley Toke; his words of reassurance saved the day, at least for the moment. 'No worries there, Marley. You can come and stay on my boat with me if Marcia Whatsit chucks you out. I'll clear some of my junk out of the old spare cabin, and as long as you keep the cakes coming, you can stay until you get fixed up with something better.'

Hettie marvelled at Poppa's kind offer. She knew how much he loved his independence. On the day his old uncle Ned had died—in his chair by the fire in the snug at the Tot and Towpath—Poppa had become the proud owner of *The Ned-Do-Well*, a forty-foot narrow boat which had given him a home of his own and a place from which to run his plumbing business. He lived happily there, enjoying his own company and pleasing himself, and his offer of a bolt-hole for Marley was generous in the extreme.

'Poppa boy! You a very fine cat, savin' me bacon,' Marley said, cheering up instantly. 'I'll keep Moggy's tings safe in me room for now, but de old mother cat needs to know dat Moggy is gone or she'll just keep writin' to the post office.'

Hettie could only imagine how Lavender Stamp would react to a mountain of uncollected mail, but agreed that something would have to be done. It was really Marcia Woolcoat's problem; Hettie's problem was deciding which bits of the sorry tale to report back to her. It was nearly five o'clock, and she couldn't put it off any longer. She left Poppa to finish his third slice of cake, collected a careful selection of Digger Patch's blackmail notes from the safety of Marley's kitchen, and—with a deep breath—made her way down the hallway to Miss Woolcoat's parlour. The door was closed. Hettie raised her paw to knock, then changed her mind and hurried back to Marley's kitchen; it was not her job to cover up the sins of others, and it suddenly occurred to her that there was another way of dealing with the situation she found herself in. She snatched up Alma Mogadon's shoebox of letters and retraced her footsteps, this time making her presence felt with a resounding thump on Marcia Woolcoat's door.

Marcia Woolcoat tested the hinges by throwing the door open with such force that she all but fell into the corridor. 'Ah, Miss Bagshot—I trust you have some news for me? I always like to enter a weekend with the trials of the week dealt with and on the way to being forgotten. Do sit down.'

Hettie was more than a little taken aback by the matron's words—she seemed to have forgotten that there was an unburied corpse on the premises—but she was getting used to her strange behaviour and decided to plough on regardless. 'Miss Woolcoat, I have completed my search of your sis . . . er . . . Nurse Mogadon's room, and have found a number of things that help to explain her decision to end her life. She was, as I suspected, being blackmailed by one of your residents, and I am now able to confirm that this was Mr Patch, your gardener.' Hettie paused, waiting for a reaction; when none came, she continued. 'Mr Patch had been sending some very unpleasant letters to Nurse Mogadon for some time, and these letters—which I have here—also contain a number of unkind rumours about your other guests. I think it best if you read them yourself.' She pushed Digger Patch's notes onto the table next to the empty lemon drizzle plate, but still Marcia Woolcoat showed no interest. 'It would appear that Mr Patch has been stealing from your clients' caskets before they were buried. Nurse Mogadon had discovered this and was going to inform you, but—as is now very clear—she had become involved in a deceit far worse than stealing trinkets, and had sold the bodies of your last three Dignicat clients to an outsider. Digger Patch knew this and threatened to expose her to get his own back. Sadly, she could see no other way out, and chose to kill herself rather than admit to you what she had done.'

Hettie had no idea if her words had hit home. Marcia Woolcoat stared straight ahead, seemingly composed and unmoved, and her attitude was beginning to unnerve Hettie a little—but the shoebox was becoming heavier by the minute, and it was time to hand it over and run. 'I found this under Nurse Mogadon's bed,' she said. 'I have only glanced at the contents, but I've seen enough to know that these are family letters which are of no interest to anyone but you. They may provide some reasons for your sister's behaviour.' Feeling very brave at having used the word 'sister', and relieved that there had been no visible explosion from the cat sitting opposite her, Hettie gently rested the shoebox on Marcia Woolcoat's knee and stood up to leave. 'I will, of course, continue my investigations into who bought the bodies—if you would like me to. Perhaps you could phone my office on Monday after you've had a chance to look through the letters, and let me know how you would like me to proceed. I will obviously put all my other cases on hold until I hear from you.'

At last there was a response, but it was not what Hettie had expected. Marcia Woolcoat rose from her sofa, knocking the shoebox and its contents onto the floor. She shuffled through the letters as she moved across the room to her desk, where she located her cheque book and proceeded to write out a money order, signing it with a flourish before handing it to Hettie. 'Miss Bagshot,' she said after a pause, 'I am indebted to you and I hope this will cover your costs, and more especially your silence, in the matters you have just brought to my attention. I have no wish to continue this investigation any further, or to tie up more of your time. Please accept this cheque as final payment for your services. Now, you must excuse me—it's nearly time for the six o'clock news.'

With that, Marcia Woolcoat strode out of her room and disappeared down the corridor, leaving Hettie to see herself out.

Too shell-shocked even to look at the cheque, Hettie made her way to the front door, collected her great coat from its hook and strode out into the car park, where Poppa was waiting patiently in his twin-wheel base transit van. She climbed into the cab beside him, still holding the cheque and still not daring to look at how much it was for, but hoping that Marcia Woolcoat had remembered the bonus that had been promised for a satisfactory outcome. Admittedly, Hettie was unable to pinpoint anyone in the Furcross case who could truly be described as satisfied by the service she had provided; in fact, since she had arrived on Wednesday, everything had got a whole lot worse. As she and Poppa drove away, narrowly missing Digger Patch who sat on his suitcase at the bus stop, she wondered if she was entirely cut out for the work she had chosen. Her doubts vanished when she finally glanced down at Marcia Woolcoat's cheque, and saw in disbelief that it had been made out for fifty pounds.

The rush hour traffic in the high street was

heavier than usual. Oralia Claw's van had obstructed the departure of Turner Page's mobile library, which now seemed to be wedged across the road, forcing Lavender Stamp—who had been directing the traffic—up against the Butters' shop window. Poppa took decisive action and jumped the queue of traffic by taking to the pavement on the post office side of the street. Seeing his success, the rest of the cars followed suit and it soon became clear that Oralia Claw, Turner Page and Lavender Stamp would be going nowhere for the time being. Hettie was grateful for Poppa's swift response to the hold-up: she was long past her best on a day that had started at three o'clock in the morning with a hysterical Jamaican cook, and had expanded into a room search with a corpse for company, an unpleasant interrogation with a burnt-out celebrity gardener, and a surreal encounter with Marcia Woolcoat brandishing a cheque for fifty pounds. The cheque now shared a pocket with a squashed samosa, Hettie having hurriedly stowed it away in case Marcia Woolcoat ran after them and asked for it back. She was dead on her paws and, as she waved Poppa on his way, her only thought was of a blazing fire and her comfortable old armchair. She had had no time to consider that—for the first time in her life—she was financially secure. In spite of her haphazard approach, it seemed that she was a successful detective after all.

CHAPTER TEN

Tilly knew that whatever had befallen Hettie at Furcross, she would have had one of her 'difficult' days, so she made all the homecoming preparations before setting to work on the agency's rate sheet. A battle of wits between Tilly and the typewriter had been raging for some time when Hettie finally fell through the door. The problem—as far as Tilly could see—was that the typewriter had been blessed with a mind of its own, and that particular mind was a tetchy and spiteful one. She had done her best to make friends with it, coaxing it into life by gently tapping its keys and not being too harsh with the carriage return lever, but all she got for her consideration was badly spelt words, numbers where there should have been letters, and holes in the paper where the arms had pressed too hard. To make matters worse, it had decided to unravel its ribbon, covering everything in red and black ink, including Tilly. If the typewriter had been given a voice, it might have suggested that Tilly's paws were simply too wide for the job and that it could not be expected to choose from three letters every time she hit a key; it might also have gone on to point out that the typist was in charge of the spelling, and that a typewriter's job was merely to supply the letters and the mechanical action to get them onto the page. Mercifully, the machine had *not* been given a voice, and Tilly remained oblivious to her shortcomings, assuming that she and this particular wordsmith simply did not get on. It was only in the last few minutes that the machine had seen fit to spew out something vaguely recognisable as a price list. As she appraised her ink-stained offering, even Tilly had to admit that it needed a bit more work, but she had made a start and that—in her book—was the main thing.

With much tugging and pushing, the typewriter was returned to its place under the desk, which was halfway through its transformation into supper table when Hettie stumbled over the threshold under the weight of her day. Tilly skipped to the door and helped her off with her coat, seeing instantly that the visit to Furcross had offered a number of challenges; by the tired look on Hettie's face, a good supper was needed as soon as possible. She put a match to the fire, which responded instantly, and Hettie—not wishing to crumple her warm business slacks—exchanged them for her dressing gown, pulling the samosa and the cheque out of the pocket before abandoning her day clothes in the second drawer of the filing cabinet. The cheque was tossed like an old shopping list onto the staff sideboard and the samosa—a little worse for wear but still recognisable—was placed on Tilly's fireside blanket for later. Tilly busied herself setting out their supper, keeping half an eye on her friend's silent, methodical dismantling of her day; she was desperate to hear the latest news on the case, but she knew that Hettie would speak when she was ready.

She had to wait longer than she hoped: Hettie climbed into her armchair and, with a grateful sigh and a yawn that threatened to consume the hearth, fell into a deep sleep as the fire filled their little room with the shadows of dancing flames. Hunger woke her eventually and, with one eye open, she noticed that Tilly had changed into her pyjamas and was resting on her blanket by the fire with her nose stuck firmly in the latest Polly Hodge mystery. A slight turn of the head told her that the gingham tablecloth on her desk was laden with an untouched supper and, for the first time that day, all seemed to be well.

'What's in the pies?' asked Hettie, stretching her tabby paws out in front of her.

Tilly jumped, startled at the break in the silence, and tore herself away from a rather nasty knife murder that Polly Hodge had seen fit to include in chapter two. 'I went for the award-winning sausage and onion, but then I thought—what if we don't like it? So I got your favourite steak and kidney as well. And there's cream horns for pudding.' Hettie purred with satisfaction, and gave her paws and face a cursory lick as Tilly added some coal to the fire and put the kettle on. She struggled from her chair and cut the two pies in half; examining the sausage and onion filling, and deciding that it looked very good indeed, she put half of each pie on the two plates that Tilly had laid out for them. As they ate, she went through the events of the day, encouraged by Tilly's occasional gasps and mild expletives to wring every ounce of drama out of what would always be known as the 'Furcross Case'. When the pies had been dispatched, they returned to their fireside to suck the life out of Beryl Butter's cream horns and Hettie loaded her catnip pipe, settling back in her chair to wait for Tilly's questions and for the wisdom which she would no doubt bring to the mystery. Marcia Woolcoat's three pounds had been excitedly stowed away in the rainy day tin on the mantelpiece, empty and neglected in recent months, but Hettie had not yet mentioned the cheque. In the true tradition of the command performance, she was saving the best until last.

'What do you think Marcia Woolcoat will do when she's read the shoebox letters?' asked Tilly, scraping cream off the spine of her book. 'It might send her mad. Then she might go on a killing spree, or set fire to Furcross with all the cats still in it.'

Tilly's enthusiasm built to a crescendo, inspired by Polly Hodge to include as many classic scenarios as she could remember, and Hettie marvelled at her friend's imagination, knowing that Marcia Woolcoat was probably capable of all of them. 'I think Miss Woolcoat's world is crumbling around her ears,' she said, when Tilly had run out of dramatic endings. 'Her problems started long before she set up Furcross, and I think her chickens are all coming home to roost at once. When I left, she seemed more dead than her sister, and she certainly wasn't interested in taking the case any further—which is a shame, because we could have got another week's work out of her.' Hettie said the last few words with a twinkle in her eye, then a broad grin, and Tilly put the change of demeanour down to the catnip until Hettie sprang from her chair and snatched the folded piece of paper from the staff sideboard. 'She did give me this, though. What do you make of it?'

She allowed the cheque to float down onto Tilly's blanket and watched as her friend unfolded the paper and read the glorious words over and over again, vocalising the sum in a mystic chant. 'Fifty pounds. Fifty pounds. How can it be for fifty pounds? Look! It says "Pay Miss Bagshot the sum of fifty pounds", and she's signed it. Look! It says Marcia Woolcoat. How can there be so much money on one piece of paper?' Tilly stood up and danced around her blanket, grinding flaky pastry and samosa crumbs into the carpet, and for the first time Hettie felt the joy of their windfall. She joined Tilly in her dance and they spun round the room together, without a care in the world.

Exhausted but happy, they fell into their beds and Tilly entertained Hettie with the highlights of her day: first her encounter with a video cassette, and then her triumphant visit to Jessie's shop and the three new best cardigans. Hettie was in too good a humour to calculate just how long her office cat had been missing from her post, and promised to look in at the shop the next day in case Tilly got busy and needed help. As they drifted off to sleep, they chatted about the evening at Malkin and Sprinkle, wondering who would be there and—now that Tilly had settled on her new blue cardigan—what Hettie would wear. The question remained unanswered as they fell asleep in the warm glow of the dying fire.

CHAPTER ELEVEN

Several hours later, Tilly awoke with a start and shook Hettie urgently out of a dreamless sleep. 'Wake up! Wake up! It's no good! It's just a piece of paper! We can't spend it!'

Hettie opened both eyes as Tilly's whiskers tickled her face. She sat up and blinked. 'Whatever's the matter? Are we on fire? Have the Butters' ovens done for us?' She looked at the anxious expression on her friend's face and pulled her dressing gown around her shoulders.

'I was having a lovely dream about TV sets. We were going to buy the biggest one in the shop and you gave them Miss Woolcoat's cheque, but the cat serving us just laughed and said it was only a bit of paper and we'd have to have proper money if we wanted a television.' Hettie listened carefully and, to her horror, came to the same conclusion as the cat in Tilly's dream: the cheque was worthless unless they could get it cashed for proper money. 'You'll have to open a bank account,' Tilly continued, 'and you'll have to do it in the morning because it's Saturday and they shut at twelve.'

Hettie knew there wasn't a bank in the High Street that would allow her to open an account. During her music days, she had become rather overdrawn at several of them and had gained a reputation for being somewhat unreliable. The fact that she had eventually paid off the debts didn't seem to matter to the fat cats who swivelled round in their chairs, puffing on their cigars and encouraging the overdrafts, then pulling up the drawbridge when they'd squeezed an extortionate amount of interest out of the financially challenged. Hettie had vowed never to enter a bank again, deciding that if fortune ever came her way she would keep it in notes under her armchair, but as usual Tilly was right: Marcia Woolcoat's cheque meant nothing unless it could be cashed. 'I can't go to the bank,' she admitted. 'They won't have me. The only way to sort this out is to go back to Furcross and ask Marcia Woolcoat for cash instead of a cheque, but the last time I saw her she was positively suicidal and I'm not sure I can go through all that again.'

'What about the post office?' asked Tilly. 'Have they blacklisted you as well?'

Hettie thought for a moment. Except for the odd disapproving look from Lavender Stamp, she couldn't recall any problems with the post office, and it would be convenient to have their money just across the road where they could keep an eye on it. She nodded in a problem solved sort of way and Tilly went back to her blanket, relieved that—should she return to the TV shop in her dreams—she would be able to complete the sale with the help of Hettie's new post office savings book.

CHAPTER TWELVE

Saturday dawned bright and sunny, and both Hettie and Tilly awoke refreshed and ready to do battle at the post office counter. There was no real breakfast to be had as there had been no real money to purchase supplies before Marcia Woolcoat boosted their economy, but their dinner vouchers wouldn't be needed thanks to the free meal at Malkin and Sprinkle that evening. It was decided that—if all went well at the post office—they would indulge themselves in two of the Butters' Saturday specials, a giant bap filled with bacon and sausages and a frothy coffee in a paper cup.

Lavender Stamp had worked in the High Street Post Office since she was tall enough to reach the counter, and before that her mother Rosemarie had allowed her to watch the transactions perched on a high stool. She had learnt to count and do the most complicated arithmetic before most kittens left nursery school, and she had always expected to become postmistress when Rosemarie Stamp retired. Rosemarie had been well loved by the High Street community and, when the time came for her to stand down and move to a cottage by the sea, there was much speculation about Lavender's suitability for the job. The concerns had nothing to do with the intricacies of day-to-day business, but with the way that Lavender herself behaved towards her customers. To say that she had an unfortunate manner was being kind; in fact, to join one of Lavender's long queues signalled a willingness to be subjected to a third-degree interrogation from behind the grille, even if you required nothing more than a stamp. Those who had been part of the community for some years agreed that Lavender's sweet nature had disappeared on the day she was jilted by Laxton Sprat, a college cat who worked one summer at the sorting office and collected the mail each day. Lavender would position herself on the pavement next to the postbox, fluttering long eyelashes at Laxton as he piled the letters into his sack. Eventually he asked her out, but after some unpleasantness on the back row at the Roxy Cinema, Laxton decided to hightail it back to college a week early. To make matters worse, Lavender caught a serious infestation of fleas from the Roxy and scratched her way through the rest of that very hot summer, broken-hearted and just plain cross. The heartbreak dwindled as the flea treatment began to work, but Lavender's anger at being cast aside by a student remained, surfacing every day as she greeted her customers with the welcoming word 'NEXT!'

Hettie usually sent Tilly to the post office, as she was much more patient and far less frightened of Lavender Stamp. Tilly liked to see the good in everyone and she enjoyed licking stamps, so the ordeal usually had a nice bit at the end of it. But today was different and the two cats joined Lavender's queue together, expecting a rough ride. They were not disappointed. The post office contained none of the customer comforts enjoyed during Rosemarie Stamp's time: the row of chairs for older cats had been removed to offer more space for queueing, and the rack of colourful greetings cards was reduced to a very poor selection—the sort of card you might grab for a cat you hardly knew but felt sorry for. Lavender had discovered that the mark-up on greetings cards was derisory, and had decided to run her stock down to make way for more lucrative items, all of which were safely stowed away behind her counter, safe from shoplifters. There was, however, one curious break with the mean, sparse shopkeeping philosophy: a display case full of hand-knitted cat dolls, all in sombre colours and dressed according to their professions. There was a chimney sweep, a soldier, a sailor and even an undertaker, all lined up as if Lavender had spent her evenings knitting perfect male cats to compensate for the real one who didn't share her fireside. Each doll boasted a luggage label price tag, and the display cabinet itself proudly informed everyone that these were 'Hand-crafted, highly collectable knits by Miss Lavender Stamp'. As the queue shuffled slowly forward, Tilly gave the contents of the cabinet a good once-over, imagining what it would be like if they all came to life when the post office was closed and held Lavender to ransom behind the counter; no one in the town would pay up, and the thought made her giggle.

There was now only one cat ahead of them, and Marcia Woolcoat's cheque was getting hotter and hotter in Hettie's paw. She licked her lips nervously, wishing there was more than one post office in town and feeling sorry for the cat at the front of the queue, who was getting a dressing-down for obscuring the address on her parcel with sealing wax. After much tutting, the package was grudgingly weighed and viciously stamped, and the cat fled outside in a flood of tears, much to the distress of the rest of the queue, who knew their turn would come.

When the walls resounded to the cry of 'NEXT!', Tilly pushed Hettie forward, tucking herself behind her friend and out of the postmistress's sightlines. 'I'd like to open an account,' Hettie began, hoping that a straightforward request would be the best policy. As she dared to look through the winged diamante spectacles that adorned Lavender Stamp's otherwise plain face, she realised that her opening gambit was not necessarily the one that would cause her least pain.

'We would all like to open an account,' Lavender responded in a voice that would carry to the back of any theatre. 'To hold an account at this post office is a privilege. It is not available to just anyone who walks in off the High Street.' Lavender reached behind her and selected a form from her vast array of official applications. 'You will need to complete form POLS/SA/AC/7B, and I warn you now that if you are unable to answer any of the questions, or if you fill in any of the boxes incorrectly, you will have to start again.' Hettie looked down at the form that Lavender pushed towards her, and the post office queue fell silent, waiting for her next move. Tilly held her breath and sidled closer to Hettie's back, sheltering herself from the inevitable fall-out.

'Do you have a pen I could borrow?' asked Hettie brightly in her best posh accent. Seeing the sulphur rise from the top of Lavender's head as the postmistress morphed into one of Dante's tormented souls, she wished she had just taken form POLS/SA/AC/7B and run. The rest of the queue shrank back a little, distancing itself from the bomb that was about to go off.

Lavender had the complete attention of her audience, and she rose splendidly to the occasion. 'May I remind you—and all who are assembled here—that this is a post office. I sell stamps, postal orders, brown paper, string, cellotape, sealing wax and three sizes of envelope, and I offer a number of official documents, including vehicle tax road licences. BUT! I do not, repeat *not,* lend or sell pens. If you wish to buy a pen, I suggest that you go to a stationer's rather than waste my time by asking for items that I have no intention of stocking.' Lavender pulled the form back under the grille as if she had changed her mind about letting Hettie have it in the first place, and continued to offer a run-down of her regulations. 'To open a savings account at this post office, you will need a minimum initial deposit of one pound, a permanent address, proof of identity at that address, details of your next of kin—that's the cat you wish to leave your money to when you die— and a personal recommendation from an upright and trusted member of the community who has known you for more than three months.' Looking Hettie in the eye, Lavender seemed satisfied that she would not be able to meet any of the criteria, and was just about to shout 'NEXT!' when Hettie pushed her crumpled cheque across the counter in a final desperate bid to secure the money. Lavender shrank back from the curry smell that permeated the paper, horrified by the visible traces of Marley Toke's samosa, and unfolded the note as if it had once belonged to a plague victim. As she read the sum written on the cheque, it was her turn to gasp, and the queue edged forward as one, eager for news.

Lavender moved closer to her protective grille and lowered her voice so that only Hettie could hear. 'Miss Bagshot. I assume this is your cheque?'

Hettie nodded and Lavender continued. 'As the sum is more than ten pounds, I find myself able to offer you what I call my Premium Saver's Account. If you are able to keep a balance of no less than twelve pounds in the account at all times, I will be able to issue you with a red saver's book as soon as the cheque has cleared. Under those circumstances, you will only need to fill in form PS/01, which simply requires your name, address and a signature.' Lavender reached for the form and, taking her own pen, filled in the details under Hettie's instruction and passed the form—and pen—over to Hettie for her signature. 'If you return on Wednesday after the cheque has cleared through Miss Woolcoat's bank, I will be able to issue you with your passbook.' She stapled the cheque to the completed form with a resounding crack and rammed the paperwork onto the 'dealt with' spike, then resumed her position of High Street tyrant. 'NEXT!'

Hettie and Tilly danced triumphantly back outside, leaving Lavender Stamp and her line of victims behind. Tilly returned to their room to get ready for her stint in Jessie's shop, and Hettie joined the Butters' queue for their well-earned treats. The atmosphere was in stark contrast to the one she had just left: the smell of freshly baked bread, combined with the sweetness of cream cakes and the added bonus of Betty's breakfast griddle, gave the assembled hopefuls a joyous experience as they filed first past the savoury pie selection, then cakes and pastries, and finally a stunning array of breads and rolls, eventually reaching the counter spoilt for choice and eager to spend. A constant stream of greetings and jolly banter came from the counter end, as Betty and Beryl handled their customers' orders efficiently, while seeming to have all the time in the world. Hettie exchanged her luncheon vouchers with Beryl, who found her a tray to put the baps and coffees on, then waved her through to the back with a wink, saving her the bother of going out into the street with her precious cargo.

Tilly could smell the breakfast approaching long before she heard Hettie's footsteps in the back hall, and opened the door ready to receive their Saturday specials. 'Ooooh lovely!' she purred, fastening a tea towel round her neck to protect the best red cardigan with hood and pockets that she'd selected for her afternoon of shopkeeping. Hettie cautiously cut her lunch into four bite-sized pieces and began to chew thoughtfully, but Tilly launched herself wholeheartedly upon her own bap, holding it down with one of her large paws as she nibbled, licked and chewed until there was nothing left but a greasy memory on their gingham tablecloth. The coffee eventually left its mark, too, as she forced her face into the paper cup, determined to remove every last drop of froth and ending up with it all over her ears and the top of her head.

Hettie glanced at the clock on the staff sideboard, then at the very silent transistor radio next to it. 'I'll walk down the High Street with you when you go to Jessie's,' she said. 'I have to get some batteries for the radio or we'll miss our show tomorrow.' Tilly nodded enthusiastically, wondering if Elizabeth Traybake had ever enjoyed a sausage and bacon bap or, for that matter, liked her coffee frothy. The star with the topaz eyes had fascinated her since the day she found a biography in the old library. She had read that Miss Traybake had three passions in life: diamonds, Tom cats, and cardigans—which had instantly created a bond between her and the movie star. Her adoration was cemented forever when she went to see *Cleopatra* with Jessie, and witnessed her favourite scene of all time: Elizabeth Traybake entering Rome as the Egyptian queen, dressed in a gold lamé cardigan.

'Come on—we'd better get going if you're to be on time for Jessie,' Hettie said, taking her best mac from the back of the door. 'I think it's going to rain later, so you'll need an umbrella.' Tilly grabbed the umbrella out of a pot by the door and stopped dead as Hettie struggled into her coat, only to discover that she had either put on a stone in weight or that something terrible had happened to her mac since she last wore it. 'This is ridiculous! I can't even do it up. And look at the sleeves! They're too short.'

144

Marshall County Public Library

270-527-9969

Checked out to Patricia A Garland
(29969000907748)
07/22/2017 11:32

Checked Out

Killer jam
Barcode: 34275000456875
Date due: **08/05/2017 23:59**

The No. 2 Feline Detective Agency
Barcode: 34275000457580
Date due: **08/05/2017 23:59**

You saved a total of $71.95 by using
the library to borrow these items.

Overdues

News

Tilly could only stare in horror. Realising what had happened, she burst into tears. 'It was me,' she sobbed. 'I was only trying to help. I knew how upset you were about the mud and the piccalilli, so I washed it myself because we couldn't afford the dry-cleaners. Then I wore it to go to Jessie's, as it wasn't quite dry. It was meant to be a nice surprise and now it's ruined!'

Tilly's sobs got louder until she noticed that her friend was laughing as she struggled out of the mac. 'Well, there's only one thing for it,' said Hettie, trying to keep a straight face. 'I'll just have to buy a new one. And as for you!' Tilly closed her eyes and waited to be given her marching orders. 'If the mac fits, then you'll have to wear it—on special missions and that sort of thing. After all, detectives need macs so they can turn their collars up and look suspicious under street lamps.'

Tilly couldn't believe what she was hearing. 'If I have a mac, does that mean I can be a real detective like you?'

'Of course you can. Now we've solved our first case, I think we need to look the part—and you are my official sidekick, after all. You'll need a mac to keep your notepad and pencil in, just in case you have to jot something down when we're out on a job.'

Tilly's eyes grew as big as saucers at the prospect of being Hettie's official sidekick; she had never been official in her life, and this wasn't the moment to point out that the case hadn't been solved, exactly. The two cats strode off down the High Street, Tilly feeling extra important in her new detective mac and Hettie settling for an umbrella until she could access her savings account to go shopping. The rain had started by the time they parted company outside Meridian Hambone's hardware shop, and Hettie headed inside in search of batteries.

The Hambones had kept a shop on the High Street for over a hundred years and Meridian looked as if she'd been there right from the start, although she could still climb to the top shelves when the need arose. Her shop was the cheapest in the town for just about everything, from sink plugs to tins of paint, and her toothless grin was always welcoming. Hettie loved Hambone's because it maintained an old-world charm that was rare and inviting. The shop smelt of firelighters, wood and turpentine—and so did Meridian, perched on a high stool by the counter, chewing her way through a jar of wine gums and occasionally spitting the ones she didn't like into a bucket by the till. She had been a raven-haired beauty in her day and a favourite with the visiting gypsy Toms who brought the fair to town; they had left her with more than candy floss when they moved on, and Meridian had lost count of how many kittens she had brought into the world, but she had loved them all. Now, in her old age, the wicked twinkle that had got her into so much trouble was still there and her saucy innuendos made even her younger, more streetwise customers blush.

Hettie made her way to the far end of the shop, getting a welcoming flash of gums from Meridian on her way past. The section she was looking for included some of Hambone's larger, more expensive items, all looking more than a little shop-soiled and falling under the banner of 'Electrics'. It was no secret that Meridian sourced her 'Electrics' from the backs of lorries, but her customers were grateful for her enterprising nature as the questionable pedigree of the items was reflected in their price. There was a Hoover, a collection of dusty electric fires, a record player with detachable lid, a radiogram in a roll-top cabinet (slightly bashed), and several television sets of varying size. As Hettie located the batteries next to the torches and kettles, she noticed a video machine and remembered Tilly's description of her close encounter with a cassette in the library van. She was just wondering if Marcia Woolcoat's cheque would stretch to a 'back of a lorry' TV when she heard raised voices from the front of the shop.

'Get off me yer devils!'

'Stay still you stupid old cat or my friend 'ere will slit yer throat from ear to ear.'

Hettie shrank back behind the kettles, then—remembering she was a detective—made her way

147

slowly and quietly back up the centre aisle towards the counter. She paused by the mops, buckets and sponges to take in the scene in front of her: two nasty-looking Tom cats were by the till, one of them holding Meridian captive with a knife at her throat, the other emptying the day's takings into a bag. Hettie moved swiftly into the gardening section and armed herself with a spade, then took a deep breath and gave out an ear-piercing yowl as she ran towards the counter wielding the spade in front of her. The Tom with the knife was startled long enough for Meridian to wriggle free of his grip and slide under the counter as Hettie waded in with her weapon—first, a sharp jab to the knife cat, then one swift blow to knock the money thief senseless. The contents of Meridian's till scattered across the counter and, as the rolling change settled, Hettie retrieved the knife from the floor and Meridian from under her counter. She settled the frightened shopkeeper on a floor cushion from soft furnishings, keeping half an eye on the two robbers.

Gradually, the Tom cats regained their senses and squirmed on the floor, nursing their battered heads as Hettie loomed over them with her spade and knife. Only now did she begin to take in the enormity of what had just happened, and how brave and foolhardy she had been, and the knowledge made her tremble. She had barely recovered when the shop door was flung open by a large cardboard box, followed by a giant of a cat. 'Hello Ma! Sorry I'm late, but I got some good st . . . Hey! What's goin' on?' The cat looked at his mother on her cushion, then made a lunge for Hettie, who successfully sidestepped him. As he crashed to the floor, he noticed that he had joined a fast-growing band of casualties, finally putting two and two together as he eyed up the robbers.

Lazarus Hambone rose to his feet and gallantly relieved Hettie of her weapons. 'Come on now, I'll deal with them. You look after Ma.' He led her away from the counter, finding another cushion and placing it next to Meridian's, and Hettie— grateful and still shaking—took her place on the floor in what had become the recovery area of the shop. Lazarus helped himself to two lengths of strong rope from the chandlery section and bound the robbers together. He dragged them away from the counter, parking them in Meridian's paraffin and oil department. 'There you are! That should hold yer till I've sorted me Ma out. I shall have a bit of fun with you two later—we'll be goin' on a little drive, so don't make any plans fer the rest of yer lives.' The Tom cats cowered as Lazarus bolted the shop door and returned to his mother and Hettie, who was beginning to feel a little steadier now that the danger had passed.

'That's my boy!' croaked Meridian, looking up at her son and turning to Hettie. 'And to think I nearly threw 'im out with the rubbish when he was born—sickly runt of me litter, thought he was dead. I was wrappin' 'im up in a bit o' newspaper and he gives out the biggest yowl as the life comes back into 'im. That's why I calls 'im Lazarus, risen from the dead 'e was.' Lazarus looked embarrassed as his mother launched into their family history, and cut her short by offering his paw to Hettie as she struggled from the cushion, keen now to pay for her batteries and leave the crime scene behind.

'You can't let her go yet,' protested Meridian. 'She's saved me life! That ugly one would 'ave slit me throat if she 'adn't smacked 'im. Get her whatever she wants. You pick something nice from me 'lectrics, dearie.' Meridian encouraged Hettie with her broadest gummy smile as Lazarus returned to his captives to check that the ropes were secure.

Hettie knew exactly what she wanted from Meridian's ' 'lectrics' and wasted no time in making her request. 'Well, if it's not too much to ask, I would love one of your TVs, and perhaps a set of batteries for my radio?' Hettie thought she might have pushed her luck with the batteries, but tried anyway and was delighted with the response.

'Gawd love us! Chuck that video thing in as well,' Meridian squawked at Lazarus. 'Take 'er down and get 'er to pick out a telly, and get it all delivered to 'er door.'

Hettie followed Lazarus to the back of the shop as Meridian scrambled to her feet and began to collect up the notes and coins that had been scattered during the assault, giving both robbers a hefty whack on the shins with her walking stick as she tottered past them. Hettie wished that Tilly could have been with her to choose their TV—it was such a nice thing to do, and Tilly was so much better at keeping pace with technology—but she did remember one of the things that Tilly had mentioned about the 'beastly video thing', as she put it, and hoped that Lazarus could help. 'Are all these TVs compatible with this video machine?' she asked, impressed by how knowledgeable she sounded. 'I understand that some of them don't get on.'

Lazarus thought for a moment, looking as lost as Hettie, then he brightened. 'I tell yer what— my mate Poppa knows all about this stuff, so why don't I get him to bring it round and set it up for you? It's the least I can do. Would Monday suit?'

Hettie laughed out loud, and—seeing the puzzled look on Lazarus Hambone's face—responded gratefully. 'Yes, Monday would be perfect. Thank you.' She chose her batteries, collected the umbrella which she had leant against the Hoover, and bid Meridian—who had regained her perch and her wine gums—a cheery goodbye, emerging into the High Street just as the heavens opened and the rain poured down. Putting her umbrella up, she decided to pay a call on Tilly at work, and smiled all the way there.

CHAPTER THIRTEEN

While Hettie was wielding a garden spade at two of the town's less desirable types, Tilly headed to Cheapcuts Lane to languish in the delights of Jessie's charity shop. Jessie gave her the guided tour as they shared a round of sardines on toast and, once the cash till had been mastered, Tilly brought her up to speed on the Furcross case and her own new status as Hettie's official sidekick. Jessie was impressed and pleased for Tilly; she knew that Miss Lambert would be smiling down proudly at Tilly's advancement, and told her so before she set out for Malkin and Sprinkle to join the backstage chaos that was Cocoa Repel's autumn fashion event.

Tilly had never run a shop before, but knew it was a big responsibility. She sat on Jessie's chair and fidgeted, then thought she should look busy in case a customer came in. There was a box of old books under the counter that someone had donated, and she began to sort through them. Their covers were torn and sticky and they all smelt of smoke, but to Tilly they were treasure. She had never owned a book, and although the library offered her plenty to read, she always had to take them back and sometimes that was difficult. She found a couple of Polly Hodges in the bottom of the box and had just put them aside when the shop bells gave warning of her first customer. She sprang up, banging her head on the counter, and emerged looking a little dazed as a mother and three kittens bustled in and banged the door shut behind them. The kittens, thinking they had been let loose in a playground, began clambering all over Jessie's carefully colour-coded clothes rails, swinging on the scarves and playing hide-and-seek in the boxes of hats and shoes. Tilly stared in horror as the shop was turned upside down. The mother turned her back on her offspring and browsed through Jessie's winter coat selection as if the kittens were nothing to do with her. To make matters worse, the bells rang again to herald the arrival of two elderly female cats, dressed identically in full-length plastic macs, with orange headscarves tied tightly round their several chins. Their umbrellas dripped in unison across the floor as they made their way towards the skirt and blouse area, where a kitten had become entangled in a ball of wool and was crying for help. One of the twins prodded the kitten with her umbrella, making it cry even more, and the other did exactly the same, laughing at the young cat's distress. Suddenly there was a crash from the other side of the shop as a tea set leapt off the bric-a-brac shelf and smashed to pieces on the floor, revealing the other two kittens clinging to the shelf above.

Tilly never lost her temper unless it was completely worthwhile but, as she took in the carnage around her, she decided that now would be a good moment to explore the harsher side of customer relations. Taking a pair of scissors from the counter, she pushed her way through to the now screaming kitten, picked it up by one ear and proceeded to cut it out of its woollen ball; once freed, the kitten ran to its mother and hid under her skirt, still crying. Tilly then addressed the twins: 'If you wish to stay in the shop, would you please leave your umbrellas at the door. They are dripping all over the carpet, and I am not happy about my customers being prodded with them. You are both old enough to know better.' She left them open-mouthed with shock and returned to the counter, where she picked up a brush and dustpan and moved to the other side of the shop. 'I think you'll find it much easier to clean up the broken crockery with this!' she said to the mother, who was still browsing. 'And as you'll be paying for that particular tea set, I'll get you a bag to put the pieces in.' Tilly forced the brush and dustpan into the surprised cat's paws and the shop bells sounded again; this time, she danced across to the door in relief as Hettie stepped over the threshold and out of the rain.

Hettie quickly assessed that the course of true shopkeeping had not run smoothly for Tilly. By now, the elderly twins were pulling and tugging at the same skirt and spitting at each other; the crockery smashing kittens were being smacked by their mother as she trampled more of the broken tea set into the carpet; and the third kitten had wet itself, adding to the umbrella puddles on the floor. After her rescue mission in Hambone's, she couldn't help but feel that it was a case of out of the frying pan into the fire. The noise was deafening, as those who had been smacked screamed and those who were cross shouted, but Tilly—now her dander was up—did seem to be getting things under control. The kittens were rounded up and put out in the rain as their mother grudgingly swept up the broken crockery and paid for it, leaving the pieces on the counter as she left. The twin harridans had discovered two identical skirts further up the rail and—in full view of anyone brave enough to watch—were squeezing themselves into them, having cast off their wet macs and headscarves. Tilly and Hettie retreated to the relative safety of the counter, and Hettie kept a watchful eye on the pensioners while Tilly put the kettle on. The twins eventually decided on the skirts and two pairs of identical fur-lined ankle boots, synchronising the opening of their purses and the handing over of exactly the same coinage from each. Hettie felt that she should step up to the plate by providing matching carrier bags from Jessie's pile of reusables; her efforts met with a shared appreciation as the cats snapped their purses closed, picked up their bags and shuffled to the door. Once outside, Hettie couldn't help but admire their timing as both umbrellas were raised simultaneously, disappearing as one from view and leaving Jessie's shop a little richer, if somewhat picked over.

'What a nightmare,' observed Hettie as she hugged her tea. 'How on earth does Jessie put up with such odd cats treating her shop like a jumble sale every day, not to mention a nursery? She must have the patience of a saint.'

Tilly giggled at the thought of Jessie's saintliness, remembering some of the more irreverent comments that she had made regarding the Methodists across the road. 'Did you see anything nice in Hambone's?' she asked.

'Not really. Bit of a non-event,' lied Hettie, who found it almost impossible to keep a secret. 'Old Ma Hambone is still on her perch, and I had the honour of meeting one of her many sons— a giant called Lazarus, nice enough but as dodgy as the shop itself. And there was nothing that caught my eye.' She saw the joke in what she had said, but covered well by engrossing herself in a box of stray buttons on the counter.

Tilly finished her tea and tidied the skirt rail, which had received a number of direct hits from the terrible twins. The rest of the afternoon passed peacefully. Perfectly nice cats came and went, some making small purchases, others just browsing or dropping off bags and boxes of unwanted items for Jessie to sort through at her leisure. By the time Tilly came to cash up, she was pleased to see that she had taken over twelve pounds. As instructed, she carefully removed the takings and deposited them in a bank bag next to Miss Lambert on Jessie's mantelpiece in the back room. Then she and Hettie locked up for the day and posted the keys back through the letter box.

The High Street looked fresh and sparkly as the sun put in a late appearance, making the day's puddles shine like glass. As Hettie and Tilly passed Hambone's, Meridian was dragging in her display buckets, ready to shut up for the day, and she caught Hettie's arm. 'I won't forget what you done today, dearie. Us Hambones always pays our debts.'

With her now familiar smile, she retreated back into the shop and Tilly watched her go, puzzled. 'What did she mean?' she asked as Hettie quickened her step, buying herself time to answer the question.

'Oh, I just fetched a garden spade for her while she was busy at the till. I can't think why she's being so grateful, but you know what she's like. She's probably overdosed on wine gums.' Hettie could feel her ears getting redder, as they often did when her imagination ran away with her, and she hoped for once that Tilly wouldn't notice things in that mild, quiet way of hers.

As soon as they got back to their room Tilly sprang into action, dragging the tin bath from the yard and putting it in front of the fire. They took it in turns to fill and boil kettles of water until the bath was half full, and Tilly poured some washing-up liquid into the water, stirring it round to make bubbles. Hettie had never been too keen on bath night, being an advocate of the lick-and-promise school of hygiene, but it had been a taxing and difficult week and the idea of a long hot soak was beginning to appeal to her. She pulled off her clothes and tested the water, then climbed into the bath, sinking slowly down as the warm water engulfed her and sneezing as the bubbles reached her nose. Tilly took a pair of towels from one of the drawers in the staff side-board and joined Hettie. They indulged themselves for some time, one at each end, until Hettie reluctantly left the bath's comforting warmth. She wrapped a towel round her and dripped across the floor to the top filing cabinet drawer, where she kept her best clothes. With the recent excitement, she had had no time to consider what she might wear for their evening out, and—as it was a fashion event—she wanted to push the boat out.

As the fire crackled merrily away, Hettie paraded her finery, seeking Tilly's approval. First came the full length purple and gold kaftan, worn at numerous music festivals and bearing grass stains as proof; then the sailor trouser suit, complete with bell bottoms and oversized collar, which didn't seem to fit any more and was hurriedly set aside as a possible summer outfit for Tilly or, at worst, a donation to Jessie's shop. By now, Hettie was getting desperate, but then her paw fell on the matador outfit at the bottom of the drawer.

This fashion statement had been made for her several years back, when she entered the Southwool fancy dress parade and carried off first prize, having performed her paso doble on the May Queen's float after one too many glasses of something Spanish and fizzy. She struggled into the black culottes and white blouse with frilly front and back-turned cuffs, then added a bright red cummerbund which hid a multitude of sins. The final touch was a black crêpe waistcoat with red silk lining, and Tilly clapped her paws in delight as Hettie paraded round their room, giving out the occasional '*olé*' and using her bath towel as the incitement for an imaginary bull, spearing the fire with the poker as she went in for the kill.

Tilly finished her bath and ladled the water into the sink with their milk pan before laying out her new best blue cardigan and a pair of red woollen tights to complement the black patent-bar sandals that Hettie had bought for her last birthday. Twenty minutes later, they stepped out into the High Street feeling fabulous. Poppa drew up in his van, wearing black tie and looking every bit the handsome escort, and the three cats sped off into the night, full of excitement and looking forward to their free dinner at Malkin and Sprinkle.

Poppa dropped the girls off at the main entrance, leaving them to fight their way through an expectant crowd which hoped to catch a glimpse of Cocoa Repel or her movie star mother. Cocoa's fashion event had created a great deal of interest in the town, and tickets sold out instantly as the evening promised an excellent dinner, a top band and a discount on any of the garments shown. The great and the good had turned out in full force, and Hettie and Tilly were swept up the escalator to the second-floor ballroom in a wave of posh frocks and sparkling jewellery. The ballroom boasted a high-domed stained-glass ceiling with dancing cherub cats circling round it, and had a glittering beauty that was rarely noticed during normal shop hours, when the room was used as a restaurant and display area for special events. Tonight, the displays had been put away and replaced by a stage and catwalk that ran three-quarters of the way down the room. It was decorated with early autumn flowers and flanked by a host of small dining tables, laid up and ready to receive the guests.

Mr Malkin and Mr Sprinkle stood either side of the escalator to welcome everyone, while a number of their staff collected tickets and showed the audience to their tables. Hettie had no pockets in her outfit, so Tilly had been entrusted with their passes and, as they neared the top of the escalator, Doris Lean from pre-packed meats scrutinised their tickets to make sure they weren't fakes. Hettie noticed the 'what are the likes of you doing here?' look on the shop assistant's face and made a point of sharing a few extra words with Mr Sprinkle, as if they had known each other for years. When the niceties had been exchanged, Doris marched Tilly and Hettie grudgingly to a table at the bottom of the catwalk, close to a roped-off area where a small dais had been set up for the band. By now, Tilly's eyes were threatening to pop out of her head and even Hettie's mouth remained slightly ajar in the wonderment of the occasion, but she adopted a casual air for appearance's sake, and especially for the benefit of Doris Lean who—once the guests were seated—would be spending her evening in toilets and cloaks.

Tilly sat on her paws for fear of touching anything she shouldn't, and marvelled at the shiny cutlery in front of her. The snow-white napkins had been folded into conical peaks and there was a set of silver salt and pepper pots, but the best thing on the table—which held Tilly's eye for some time—was a silver dish of butter curls.

Poppa appeared minutes later, having successfully parked his van in a side street, and was just in time to partake of the first round of drinks. Tilly opted for a pink milkshake, full of bubbles and topped with cream and chocolate hundreds and thousands. Hettie and Poppa chose the more sensible option and relieved the waiter of two glasses of champagne which they downed in one, insisting on a refill before he moved on. 'Decent gig this,' noted Poppa, picking up the menu card. 'The food looks good, too. There's prawns to start, in some sort of sauce I can't pronounce, then there's pork and lamb kebabs with salad pittas and another sauce I can't pronounce.' Tilly released her paws and climbed onto the table to reach the top of her milkshake, licking the cream and chocolate off the top. Hettie discreetly drew her attention to the napkin, and Tilly did her best to wipe away her excesses as Poppa continued to entertain them with the menu. 'We've got a choice of puddings—there's creamed rice with chocolate crispies or sticky toffee pudding with a sauce I can't pronounce.'

Hettie laughed and snatched the menu away from him. 'Sauce onglaze it says—that's another word for custard, I think. And look—there's a selection of cheese and biscuits as well.' She downed her second glass of champagne and Poppa followed suit as the wine waiter passed close by, eventually responding to a rather loud hiccup that Hettie had tried to suppress. Once again he filled their glasses and, as Mr Sprinkle made his way to the podium on stage, all eyes turned in his direction.

'My dear friends and valued customers,' he began, 'it is my great pleasure to welcome you all here tonight on behalf of myself and my partner, Mr Malkin. I'm sure you know that fashion is one of the jewels in our crown, and we are very pleased to bring you the latest work of Miss Cocoa Repel—one of our most innovative designers, who is revealing her autumn collection exclusively to those assembled here this evening.' The ballroom erupted into riotous applause at the mere mention of Cocoa Repel, giving Hettie a much-needed opportunity to continue with her hiccups. Once the clapping had died down, Mr Sprinkle continued. 'To make the night go with a swing, would you please put your paws together for our resident band, fresh from their summer season on Southwool Pier. I give you, Kit Krooner and his Hot Jumpin' Sardines.' Everyone looked eagerly towards the back of the ballroom as the band members found their places and took up their instruments. 'Our chefs have surpassed themselves with tonight's menu, and food and drink will be served throughout the evening. I have also been asked to mention that Miss Oralia Claw will be featuring her accessories to complement Miss Repel's new designs, all of which will be available in store from Monday or by advance order with a discount this evening. Now—please enjoy yourselves, and let the music begin!'

With a nod to the band, Mr Sprinkle joined his family at a table close to the stage. Kit Krooner and his Hot Jumpin' Sardines were on their fourth number by the time the prawn starters arrived, giving Hettie and Tilly plenty of time to have a good look at the audience. They were pleased to recognise so many of the townsfolk. The Butters were dressed to the nines in matching sea-green evening gowns and shared their table with Lavender Stamp, who—although a little drab by comparison—looked smart and expensive. Turner Page had a table to himself and seemed a little lost among the finery, but he had made an effort and sported a bright yellow bow tie; he seemed to be doing a crossword puzzle as he waited for his dinner and tapped his paw to the music. Local newspaper veteran Hacky Redtop was making notes at the table he shared with Prunella Snap, the paper's features photographer, who had made her name in the world of modelling before falling from grace over a rather rushed airbrush job. These days, she was much happier photo-graphing weddings, guide troops and elderly cats who had reached a hundred.

Hettie scanned the tables, looking for some of the Furcross cats, and eventually found them sitting closer to the stage end of the ballroom. She recognised a number of the residents, including Nola Ledge and Nutty Slack, but there was no sign of Marcia Woolcoat or Marley Toke. Marilyn Repel was holding court at her own table, joined from time to time by Mr Malkin and Mr Sprinkle, who both asked for autographs. She wore one of her most famous movie costumes, a dress of shimmering gold with a plunge neckline, finished off by a stunning diamond necklace and white fur stole draped across her shoulders. Poppa found it hard to take his eyes off her, and couldn't resist speaking out loud what the rest of the room was thinking: 'Whatever she had, she's still got it in bucket loads.'

The prawns arrived with a flourish, still in their shells, and the waiter placed small bowls of scented water on each table for cleaning sticky paws. Tilly sipped her water, thinking it was the next round of drinks, and ate the shells as well as the prawns without any ill effect. A drum roll from the band signalled the beginning of the fashion event, and the catwalk sprang to life with a procession of tall, thin models in a colourful explosion of silk and chiffon; they danced and swirled past the delighted audience—stopping, moving on and turning this way and that, making sure that everyone got a good look at the clothes on show. Hettie used the spectacle to summon a wine waiter to replenish their glasses, and Poppa—being extra helpful—relieved another of a full bottle of champagne, which he hid under their table in case the top-ups petered out. Tilly, less interested in fizzy drinks that caused hiccups, clapped along and cheered as the mannequins paraded to the bottom of the catwalk, where they turned on their very high heels and glided gracefully back to the stage, eventually disappearing from view.

'Well, it's all very pretty,' Hettie commented, draining her glass for the fourth time, 'but why would you want to get yourself done up like that? I mean—when would you wear that stuff? It's not ideal for fetching the coal, is it?' Tilly noticed that Hettie was slurring her words and had begun to speak a little louder than normal, and put the change in her friend's demeanour down to the bubbles she was imbibing. Poppa had become completely fixated on Marilyn Repel and was about to chance his arm on an autograph request when another drum roll announced Mr Malkin's turn at the podium.

'And now to one of the evening's highlights. I am thrilled to have in our midst one of Hollywood's great stars. She has kindly agreed to perform a medley of her finest musical hits while our models prepare to reveal Miss Cocoa Repel's hat, mac and fun fur collection, so would you please welcome to the stage Miss Marilyn Repel.' The audience rose to its feet and everyone clapped with their paws above their heads as

Marilyn took Mr Sprinkle's arm and was guided through the dining tables to the band, where a tall stool and microphone awaited her. The stool proved a little tricky and Poppa sprang to her assistance, helping her haul herself and her very tight evening gown into position as the band struck up with a rousing introduction to 'Diamonds are a Cat's Best Friend'. Marilyn responded, blowing kisses to her fans before launching into the first verse, and Poppa sat at her feet and melted.

Hettie and Tilly were equally mesmerised by the cat who had transformed herself from one of Furcross's retired residents into a full-blown diva. Through a champagne mist, Hettie couldn't help but observe that Cocoa Repel would have to go to some lengths with her 'hacs, mats and fum furs' to hold a candle to her mother, who was proving to be the real star of the evening. As Marilyn crooned and the band played on, waiters moved like unseen ghosts among the tables, clearing away the debris, replenishing glasses and bringing hot, silver-domed serving dishes to the diners. Hettie couldn't resist lifting the lid on the one theywere served, only to find a sizzling hot banquet of skewered kebabs surrounded by freshly baked miniature pitta breads; she replaced the lid with a loud clang of satisfaction which almost brought Marilyn tumbling off her stool, but Poppa steadied her as she completed the last verse of 'Heatwave' and moved seamlessly into 'My Heart Belongs to Daddy'.

Suddenly and from nowhere Jessie appeared at Tilly's side and crouched low to whisper in her ear. 'Can you and Hettie come backstage with me? I've got to show you something. It's terrible, and I don't know what to do.' Jessie's voice sounded urgent and frightened. Tilly looked across the table to where Hettie was helping herself to another glass of fizzy, and realised that there was very little point in her going anywhere in her present state; she was now singing along with Marilyn in a slightly off-key sort of way, so Tilly seized the opportunity to leave the table and the noise behind and follow Jessie to the backstage area.

She found herself in a very different world from the glitz and glamour of the ballroom. Jessie led her through groups of half-clad models, preening themselves in front of mirrors and putting the finishing touches to their painted faces, chatting and squabbling excitedly as the minutes ticked by and the next round of garments waited expectantly in the dressing area. Cocoa Repel was fussing and hyperventilating in the middle of the chaos, and Oralia Claw was checking make-up and painted nails on some of the cats as they assembled, ready to be squeezed or pinned into hats, macs and fun furs.

Jessie beckoned Tilly over to the rail of garments

closest to the stage and pulled her out of sight. 'Look at these,' she whispered. 'They're Oralia's accessories to go with Cocoa's macs.' Tilly looked at the legwarmers, mittens and scarves, thinking how warm they would be when the winter came. She was about to say so, when she saw the expression on Jessie's face. 'Look closer,' her friend insisted. 'What do they remind you of?'

Tilly thought for a moment as she turned a legwarmer over in her paws. She sniffed it, then put it back with its partner. 'I think they're very clever—just like real fur. I wish I had markings like that, and look how the stripey ones match each other!' Tilly was pleased with her assessment and Jessie was pleased with Tilly, but Oralia Claw—who had been listening from the other side of the clothes rail—wasn't pleased at all. In fact, Oralia Claw was very angry indeed.

Jessie pulled Tilly closer to her and lowered her voice even further. 'They're just like real fur because that's what they are: REAL FUR! REAL CATS' FUR!'

Tilly gasped as the truth of the matter hit her. She shrank back from the pile of accessories in horror. 'Pansy, Vita and Virginia! It's them, isn't it? It's their fur. It was Oralia Claw who wanted those bodies. She's used them to make this stuff.'

Jessie nodded. 'Yes, and she's calling it fun fur. All I can say is it's a very black day for fashion, and if it gets out she'll bring Cocoa down with her. But what do we do? We have to stop the show before the audience claps eyes on this stuff and wants to buy it!'

Tilly knew that they had a matter of minutes before the next parade of garments took to the catwalk. 'We need help. You get hold of Cocoa and tell her what we've discovered, and I'll go back out front and get Hettie and Poppa to create some sort of diversion to hold things up.' Tilly moved swiftly from behind the rail of clothes and ran straight into Oralia Claw.

'That's as far as you're going tonight—you and your nosy friend from the charity shop.' Oralia Claw pushed Tilly back behind the rail and Jessie leapt to her defence, pulling the angry cat down onto the floor. Tilly seized her moment and made a run for it, as Jessie and her opponent rolled over and over in a bundle of spitting fur, much to the amazement of the models, who stood back to give the fight the space it deserved.

Tilly didn't look back. She quickly found her way to the ballroom and, as she approached her table, it became instantly clear to her that the diversion she was hoping to set-up was already well and truly underway. All eyes were turned on Hettie. Inspired by Kit Krooner and his Hot Jumpin' Sardines, and fuelled by at least three glasses of champagne too many, she had climbed onto her table and was currently reprising her

170

paso doble while conducting the band with an empty kebab skewer. Poppa was assisting by pretending to be a bull, using pitta breads for horns, and the audience clapped and cheered along as if the fashion show no longer existed Kit Krooner slowed the pace for dramatic effect and played a daring trumpet solo to herald in the Hot Jumpin' Sardines' version of the habanera, while Hettie and Poppa turned their table into a bullring, acting out the drama for the delighted crowd. Hacky Redtop moved closer to the spectacle, making furious notes as Prunella Snap captured the scene for posterity, and Tilly stood frozen to the spot, knowing it would be impossible now to attract Hettie's attention.

Suddenly, while Hettie staged her triumphant kill and Poppa rolled over on his back as the conquered bull, the crowd's gaze moved back to the catwalk. The spitting bundle of fur rolled down it, closely followed by the first appearance of Cocoa Repel. In a split second, the show was over. Jessie, scratched and bleeding, pulled away from her assailant. Oralia Claw leapt in the air with such force that she twisted badly and fell forward off the end of the catwalk—just as Hettie raised her skewer to acknowledge the death of her imaginary bull.

CHAPTER FOURTEEN

Oralia Claw was dead, of that there was no doubt: Hettie's skewer had gone clean through her heart. Once her body had been cleared away with the remnants of dinner, a shocked Hettie, Poppa and Tilly were invited to join Marilyn Repel at her table. The movie star was comforting her daughter, who sobbed not at the death of her business partner, but of her own career, now in tatters and a very long way from the Hoot Cature to which she had aspired. Hacky Redtop, realising that he had the story of a lifetime and hoping that Prunella Snap had the pictures to go with it, jotted down some names, chatted briefly with Jessie, whose wounds were being tended by Lotus Ping, and left in a great hurry to capture the front page of the *Sunday Snout*. The rest of the audience filed out quietly, foregoing dessert for the comfort of their own homes.

Mr Malkin and Mr Sprinkle ordered taxis for the stragglers, and Tilly crept backstage while no one was looking to load what was left of Pansy, Vita and Virginia respectfully into a box, hoping that there would be an opportunity to bury the fur with their bodies. As she turned to go, Cocoa Repel appeared, tear-stained and distraught.

Seeing what Tilly was doing, she put a paw on her arm. 'Thank you for taking them away. I couldn't bear to look at them now I know who they are. I've been so stupid. It was happening right in front of my eyes. I trusted Oralia, and she has ruined me.'

For the first time, Tilly saw a real person behind the celebrity of Cocoa Repel, and her heart went out to her. 'I'm sure all this will blow over in time, and look at your beautiful clothes! Those lovely macs and the floaty dresses—Oralia Claw hasn't spoilt those, has she?'

Cocoa turned to the clothes that had seemed so alive earlier in the evening; now, they hung like shapeless shrouds, a sad testament to all her shattered hopes. 'I don't see how I can carry on. I'll never live this down. As for the clothes, take what you like. They're not beautiful for me any more.' With that, the designer turned and walked away.

Tilly stood for a moment, then moved towards the rail of macs and carefully selected a navy blue one with a good upturn on the collar and lots of deep pockets. She tried it on, appreciating the warm red detachable lining. The Cocoa Repel designer mac was at least two sizes too big for her, and that was exactly what she was looking for.

CHAPTER FIFTEEN

Hettie woke with a thumping head and no real memory of how she had got home. She knew that to open even one eye would be impossible in her present state, and lay quietly piecing together the reasons for her headache and extreme nausea. The more she tried to recall the events of the night before, the more unsettled she became. She was just beginning to convince herself that it had all been a nightmare, when the thumping in her head became louder and much more urgent. In the hope that the banging would stop, she cradled her head in her paws and pulled herself further into her blanket.

'Wake up, wake up!' urged Tilly as she pulled the blanket back. 'You're famous! Look! It's all over the front page, with pictures and everything, and you're continued on pages four and five. Oh, do wake up! Beryl Butter has just brought us a copy of the *Sunday Snout*.'

Hettie lifted her head very slightly and opened one eye. 'Why are you making such a terrible noise, and what's Beryl Butter got to do with the *Sunday Snout*? We don't read it, and anyway I'm too tired for all this. My head hurts and I'll probably be sick in a minute.' Hettie pulled the blanket back over her head and Tilly, realising

174

that nothing could be done to rouse her friend until a hangover cure was found, left their room to seek advice from the Butters.

An hour later, two aspirins, a large glass of water and eventually a cup of tea brought Hettie back into the land of the living. Boosted by two rounds of toast and marmite and feeling a little better, she sat in her dressing gown and was at last able to focus on the newspaper that Tilly pushed in front of her. If she had ever believed last night's events to be a terrible nightmare, she now realised her mistake: there it all was in glorious black and white. The front page photograph was of Hettie dressed as a matador, stabbing at the air with an empty kebab skewer; the headline read 'O'LAY! BAGSHOT BAGS FUN FUR CHEAT!' and the caption invited readers to find out what happened next by turning to the inside spread. Hettie stared down at the image, hardly daring to look. The reality of what had come next terrified her.

Seeing her friend hesitate, Tilly opened the paper at pages four and five. The headline here was much bolder—'NAILED AND IMPALED!'—and it accompanied a rather indistinct photograph of Oralia Claw's last moment as she hurtled towards the deadly point of Hettie's kebab skewer. A further series of pictures accompanied Hacky Redtop's lurid description of events: Marilyn Repel singing with the band, Cocoa Repel in tears, and a bruised and scratched Jessie being tended to by Tilly and Lotus Ping. There was no doubt that Hacky had excelled himself, with able pictorial support from Prunella Snap, but it was Hettie who shone throughout the article—a fearless heroine, a dogged detective, and a champion of everyday justice. Oralia Claw, on the other hand, was painted as a bodysnatcher, a grave robber and a vicious, spiteful opportunist who had stolen bodies to skin and make into mittens. Hettie was relieved to notice that Furcross hadn't been mentioned, but she knew it was only a matter of time before Hacky Redtop was knocking at Marcia Woolcoat's door.

As she read the details, the Furcross case finally began to make sense. Oralia Claw had always been on Hettie's suspect list, but her partnership with Cocoa Repel had given her a respectability which she obviously didn't deserve. Hacky Redtop described her as coming from a family of convicted thieves and chancers, blaming her gypsy blood for her inbred ability to hoodwink the public at large. Hettie read about Oralia Claw as if she were just another criminal made infamous to sell newspapers; she found it difficult to accept that it was she, Hettie Bagshot, who had ended the other cat's life in such a bizarre set of circumstances—a gift for any newspaper reporter.

Tilly waited patiently for Hettie to finish reading

and busied herself around their room, retrieving the matador outfit from the floor where Hettie had fallen out of it. Noticing the specks of blood on the frill of the shirt, she hurriedly pushed it into their laundry bag, out of sight. Although the *Sunday Snout* had painted her friend as a heroine, Tilly knew that she would not be happy about her part in taking a life, even if the reality had been just another hapless Hettie Bagshot accident.

'I can't believe all this has really happened,' said Hettie, finally abandoning the newspaper. 'According to Hacky Redtop, I've killed Oralia Claw and brought justice to the town, helped out by my undercover agents—that's you and Jessie. It says she was a gypsy and came from a rough family. You'd never know it to see all those posh cats preening themselves in her nail bar.'

'Well, she certainly fought like a gypsy cat,' said Tilly. 'You should have seen her set about poor Jessie last night when she realised her nasty game was up. I've never seen a fight like that, and I think Jessie will have the scars to prove it. And poor Alma Mogadon died because of her. Then there's Pansy, Vita and Virginia. And I feel so sad for Cocoa Repel. She's finished, thanks to Oralia Claw. I do think the world is a better place without her.' She hoped her words would help Hettie to come to terms with things, and was about to suggest a good breakfast to lift their spirits, when from somewhere deep inside the staff sideboard there came the unmistakable sound of the telephone. Hettie nearly jumped out of her own skin as Tilly scrambled inside the sideboard and wrestled the phone off the hook. 'Hello. This is the No. 2 Feline Detective Agency. To leave a message, please press one. To speak to someone properly, please . . .'

She was prevented from going any further by Marley Toke's voice, booming in her ear. 'Oh my days, Miss Tilly! I got no time for all dat. I needs to speak to Hettie as we has a crisis. It's Miss Marcie!' Tilly backed out of the sideboard, dragging the phone behind her, and thrust the receiver urgently in Hettie's direction.

Hettie felt her headache returning as she took the call and Marley launched into a confusing outburst of the recent events at Furcross. 'She bin up all night readin' the shoebox! I bin hearin' noises. She lost de key to Moggy's room, and she say it all my fault for not returnin' it. Now she sittin' outside de door wid no Digger to break it down, an' I just tink you still got de key as you was de last one in dere.'

Hettie shook her head in sheer bewilderment as Marley rattled on and waited until the Jamaican cook had run out of steam. It was Tilly who grasped the situation first, having heard Marley loud and clear from the other side of the room. She reached for Hettie's greatcoat, which was hanging on the back of the door, and felt in its

178

deep pockets until she located a key under a pile of toffee wrappers. Waving it triumphantly, she successfully brought Marley's diatribe to an end. Hettie promised to drop the key off at Furcross around lunchtime, accepting an invitation for them to join Marley in the kitchen for her full Jamaican Sunday roast.

'Well that's all we need,' Hettie grumbled as she replaced the receiver. 'Now we've got to traipse all the way over to Furcross with a bloody key, and I haven't a clue what's been going on there—noises, shoeboxes, whatever next?! I can't see what's so urgent, unless Marcia Woolcoat is letting out her dead sister's room. Let's just hope she removes the body first! We have been invited to lunch, though.'

Tilly was pleased to see that Hettie's sense of humour was still intact, and decided to seize her moment: the prospect of an outing with a good lunch was the perfect excuse to present her gift. She had put the box containing what was left of Pansy, Vita and Virginia outside in the hall, and had placed the designer mac on top so that Hettie wouldn't see it. She had, in fact, been far too shocked and worse for drink the night before to see anything, so the secret surprise had gone unnoticed. 'I brought the stolen skins home in case we had a chance to bury them with the rest of the bodies at Furcross,' Tilly said. 'I thought it was the right thing to do.' She watched as Hettie chewed nervously on her nails and scanned their room, looking worried. 'And I spoke with Cocoa after it was all over. She was very upset, and she said I could help myself to anything I wanted from the show as she had lost heart. So I chose something nice for you.'

Tilly opened the door with a flourish and pulled in the box with the mac perched on the top. Hettie clapped her paws in delight, cheering up immediately at the sight of the most beautiful mac she had ever seen. It fitted as if it had been made for her, and an hour later the two cats stepped out into the high street, both wearing their new best macs with the collars turned up against the rain and looking every bit the detectives they had always aspired to be. Hettie carried the box containing the last glimpses of Pansy, Vita and Virginia, hoping at least to hand them over to Marcia Woolcoat for a decent burial, and they made their way to the bus stop outside Oralia Claw's nail bar. News had obviously travelled fast: the window was adorned with the words 'BODYSNATCHER', written in red paint as a lasting reminder of Oralia's sins. Hettie looked down at the box in her arms and cradled it a little tighter, as if she could protect the contents from further harm.

The bus arrived within minutes, just as the rain began to fall in buckets, and the cats clambered on and settled themselves on the back seat. The bus conductress looked familiar as she lurched her way towards them, beaming. 'Oh, what a surprise!' she said, falling forward into Tilly's lap as the bus driver slammed on his brakes. 'Oops! I'll never get the hang of this. I used to do planes, you know—serving the meals, soothing the nerves, until I missed me flight back from one of the Costas. I thought this job would be the same sort o' thing but it ain't, not with 'im drivin'.' Hettie and Tilly exchanged a look and wondered why they were being treated to the conductress's recent job history. Tilly tried to speed things along by offering a paw full of change for their tickets but the payment was refused. 'Na! I can't take money off you two. Proper heroes travel free. I'm proud to 'ave you on me bus. You wait till I tell me sister I've met you! That'll be one in the eye for 'er—she missed all the fun while she was on cloaks and toilets.'

Tilly suddenly knew why the face had seemed so familiar. 'You must be Doris Lean's sister! You're very much alike.' She did her best to be friendly but Hettie—disturbed by the fact that she had been recognised—wanted to get off the bus as quickly as possible. Ringing the bell on the handrail, she collected her box from the seat and moved forward, squeezing past their new friend on her way to the exit. Tilly followed her down the aisle until all three of them stood by the door, waiting for the next stop.

The conductress leant over to the luggage rack and retrieved her copy of the *Sunday Snout.* ' 'Ere! Do us a favour and sign this front page to Clippy Lean before you get off.' Hettie grabbed the pen that was offered and scribbled across her photo as the driver slammed on his brakes once again. This time, she parted company with the box, which slid the length of the aisle and came to a crashing halt at the back of the bus, spilling its contents everywhere. Tilly reacted faster than anyone and ran all the way down the bus, rescuing leg warmers and mittens as she went. Hettie stared after her in horror and turned on the charm to divert Clippy's attention, insisting on dedicating pages four and five as well and giving Tilly time to gather up their unconventional cargo. When she was satisfied that all the fur had been safely collected, Tilly returned to the exit. The bus driver had decided that an extra stop wouldn't do any harm, so by the time Hettie and Tilly had bid their new friend Clippy goodbye, they only had a short walk to Sheba Gardens.

'I hope it's not going to be like this all the time,' sighed Hettie as they walked. 'That conductress will never know how close she came to the actual case, with all those bits of fur flying about on her bus. Thank goodness you grabbed it all before she realised exactly what— or rather who—it was.'

Furcross looked cold and unwelcoming as they

approached the front door. There was no sign of anyone in the chairs by the window, and no vehicles in the car park. Hettie knocked loudly but they had to wait some time before Marley Toke appeared, hot and bothered from the kitchen. 'Tank de Lord! Come into me kitchen, both of you.' Marley led the way down the corridor and past the dining room where a number of the residents sat in silence, some reading papers, others knitting or just staring out into the garden. The festive atmosphere had packed up and gone, leaving behind a group of elderly cats who were too miserable to communicate with each other, and all shell-shocked after their night out at Malkin and Sprinkle.

Marley's kitchen was enough to cheer anyone up. It steamed and bubbled with the trappings of Sunday lunch: the roast beef was cooked and sitting on a carving plate, its juices running with the promise of gravy to come; there was a giant bowl of batter waiting to be poured into Yorkshire pudding tins; and as Tilly peeped through the glass door of the oven, she spotted a legion of roast potatoes, sizzling and golden. 'I don't know why I be botherin' wid all dis,' Marley said disconsolately. 'Me breakfast got left and now I can see me roast goin' de same way. No one is talkin', some of dem left early this mornin', and Miss Marcie is fit for notink. May as well hang up me tea towel now.'

Hettie looked at the cook and noticed how exhausted she was. For a black cat, she was almost pale and her clothes looked like she had slept in them; her eyes were puffy from crying. 'Do you know about last night?' Hettie asked as Marley prodded at the beef with a skewer. 'Oralia Claw turned out to be the one who paid Alma for the bodies. She got found out and died trying to escape.'

The understatement was the only way she could bear to put it, but Marley didn't seem interested in Oralia Claw or even in the beef she was prodding. 'I tell you Miss Hettie, there was noises comin' from Moggy's room last night and no one will believe me. She's come back to haunt us, and Miss Marcie, she call me wicked for sayin' it, but I seen tings before and me knows a restless spirit when me hears one. She need buryin', not just left dere to go bad. Miss Marcie tried to open de door to prove me wrong but she lost de key, and den I remembered you still had it, and now me too frightened to look and Miss Marcie, she sittin' outside Moggy's room listenin' at de door, an' she won't speak to me.' Marley wailed into her apron and Hettie—feeling the power of her new mac and the key in its pocket—strode out of the kitchen leaving Tilly to comfort the cook.

She crossed the yard, appreciating the flourishing catnip plants as she made her way to the hospital

184

block that housed Marley and the late Nurse Mogadon, then made her way down the corridor past the dispensary, coming to an abrupt halt several feet before she reached Marcia Woolcoat. The former matriarch sat slumped on the floor, surrounded by the contents of her dead sister's shoebox and talking to herself. Hettie took the key from her pocket and moved towards the nurse's door, stepping over Marcia, who seemed oblivious to the fact that she was no longer alone.

On first inspection, the room seemed just as she had left it. She had no wish to look at the corpse in the bed, so studied everything else first: the chair was still by the window, facing out across the garden; the lamp table was as she remembered it; and some of the drawers were still slightly open from her search—but something wasn't quite right. Hettie knew she would have to look at the bed eventually, but her attention was drawn back to the window and suddenly she knew what was wrong: the curtains had been pulled back to let in the light. Behind her, Marcia Woolcoat continued talking to herself. Hettie moved further into the room, shutting the door to get a more complete view—and then she froze. The sheets were turned back in a heap, and the bed was empty. She panicked, her heart beating so fast that it threatened to burst out of her chest. Slowly, she moved closer to the bed, forcing herself to look underneath, but there was no sign of the body. Her thoughts strayed to Oralia Claw: had she stolen the body as more stock for her fur factory? But that couldn't account for the noises Marley had heard last night; by then, Oralia Claw was dead. Hettie moved to the window and checked the locks; they were rusted and impossible to shift. She turned back towards the door, and then she saw her.

Nurse Mogadon had been propped up in the chair by the window, looking out into the garden. Her face was pale and her short pink and grey striped fur was almost translucent, drained of any colour she had possessed in life. Her eyes were tightly closed, just as they had been the last time Hettie saw her—but who had entered a locked room and positioned the corpse in the chair, and why? Hettie's instinct was to carry the body back to the bed where it could be decently covered, but the thought of touching a corpse that had been dead for several days brought her earlier bout of nausea back and she struggled to control it. She looked down at the carpet, focusing on the pattern, and noticed that there were crumbs everywhere around the chair; on closer inspection, she saw that the crumbs had also settled around Nurse Mogadon's mouth and whiskers, as if someone had tried to force-feed her.

Perhaps Marcia Woolcoat could shed some light on the macabre scene. After all, it was her sister, and not really Hettie's problem. With that thought,

Hettie turned towards the door, but a paw shot out from the chair. 'Please help me! I'm so thirsty. My throat is so sore.'

The voice was cracked and faltering, and Hettie stared in amazement as Nurse Mogadon struggled to be heard. 'Stay where you are!' she shouted, her panic getting the better of her. 'Don't move until I get back.' It was perhaps the silliest thing that she had said all week, as Alma Mogadon was in no fit state to go anywhere. But she certainly wasn't dead.

Hettie wrenched the door open and dragged Marcia Woolcoat to her feet. 'She's alive! Your sister is alive! Come and see!' She pushed Miss Woolcoat into the room and propelled her towards the chair where Alma sat, looking fragile and barely able to move. Hettie grabbed a blanket from the bed and threw it over her, and Marcia stood rooted to the spot, shaking in disbelief.

'I'm so sorry,' whispered Alma as her sister, regaining her composure, fell on her knees and smothered her in a hug. 'I couldn't even manage to do the decent thing. It must have been the wrong dose, and it put me into a coma. When I woke up, I thought I was dead.' Hettie left the sisters to it and found a glass in the dispensary. She filled it with water and took it back to Alma's room, giving it to Marcia to administer, and then—assuming she was no longer required— headed back to Marley's kitchen and a roast beef lunch which was guaranteed to cure even the worst bout of nausea.

The meal proved to be a joyful occasion once the residents had shuffled off to their tables, leaving Marley, Tilly and Hettie to enjoy theirs in the kitchen. Marley had taken a modest plateful to Alma's room and had even mashed a roast potato in her special gravy for Marcia to feed to her sister a teaspoonful at a time. Tilly entertained the cook with details of the Malkin and Sprinkle fashion show and the timely demise of Oralia Claw, who—much to Marley's relief—could no longer bear witness to Nurse Mogadon's involvement in the fur scandal. With Digger Patch out of the way, Marcia and Alma could start again. When Alma felt better, they would have much to discuss—not least the contents of the shoebox which revealed where Alma had kept their mother.

When Hettie and Tilly could eat no more, Marcia Woolcoat ordered them a taxi home. As they drove away from Furcross, Hettie suddenly remembered the pale face she had seen at Alma Mogadon's window. 'Bugger!' she said. 'I could have had it all wrapped up much quicker if I hadn't believed in ghosts!' Tilly looked puzzled but said nothing, content to know that their luxury ride would get them home just in time to catch Elizabeth Traybake on the radio.

CHAPTER SIXTEEN

Hettie awoke with a start as the Butters' ovens heralded the beginning of another working week. She was pleased to be back in the land of the living. Her night's sleep had been inhabited by ghouls and zombies, all rising up out of the burial ground at Furcross. Alma Mogadon's admission to under-dosing herself in her failed suicide attempt had fuelled her imagination, and the theme of the undead engulfed her dreams: cats rose from their graves, demanding reparation for having been buried alive, and the thought of Alma's bungled attempts spreading to her Dignicat clients stayed with Hettie long after the nightmare had faded. Only the smell of the Butters' first batch of bread could convince her to open her eyes.

The room was neat and tidy, and Tilly was curled up in her blanket on the rug by the long-dead fire, snoring gently. Hettie looked at her friend's sleeping face and remembered how thin and wasted she had been when she first moved in. She had brought nothing with her but a bag of cast-off rags, a bad dose of cat flu and a willingness to please in any way she could. Now, she had become central to Hettie's life and they shared everything, including the joy of a close

189

friend-ship which Hettie had found impossible to develop with any other cat. Lessons of trust and belief had been absent from Hettie's education until Tilly's optimism flooded her world with possibilities; in fact, it was Tilly's love of detective fiction that had sparked her latest idea for making a living, and—through fair means or foul—it seemed to have become a success. She stared at the two best macs hanging on the back of the door and smiled, knowing that this friend-ship could withstand anything the weather of life threw at them as long as they stuck together. Content and satisfied with her lot, Hettie gathered her blanket around her and went back to sleep.

As the clock on the staff sideboard pointed its hands towards nine, the telephone began to ring. Tilly stumbled from her rug and clambered into the sideboard, hauling the phone off its hook, but too sleepy to run through the list of options which she had now practised to perfection. 'Hello? Yes, but she's not available at the moment—she's on an undercover operation. Perhaps you'd like to call back in an hour.' Tilly replaced the receiver and backed out of the cupboard, stretching and yawning as she made her way to the kettle. 'That was Hacky Redtop. He wants to interview you. I think it'll be a four-page spread this time.' She giggled as she put the teabags in the mugs. 'He might give you your own weekly column if you play your cards right.'

The telephone rang again, and this time Hettie was closest to it. She reached inside the sideboard and dragged it out onto the floor. 'Hello? Yes, this is the No. 2 Feline Detective Agency. Stakeouts? Yes, I suppose so. What would we be looking for? You don't know until we've seen it—ah. Big footprints in the garden, you say? And have these footprints done anything? Right, they've watered your tomatoes.' Her patience was beginning to fail her but she hid it well. 'If you would like to leave your name and address, I'll put an operative onto it as soon as one becomes available. Nineteen Whisker Terrace? Yes, I know where that is. And your name? Miss Spitforce. Right.' Tilly quickly scribbled down the details as Hettie brought the conversation to an end, but the phone rang again as soon as she replaced the receiver. This time, it was a voice that Hettie recognised. 'Miss Woolcoat—what can I do for you? Saturday afternoon? Yes, I'm sure we can. Thank you— that would be lovely. We look forward to it. Goodbye.' Tilly stood poised with her pencil and notepad, waiting for the details of the call. 'Just write down "tea at Furcross",' said Hettie, looking puzzled. 'We've been summoned on Saturday afternoon to a "thank you celebration". That should be interesting, and Marley's bound to put on a good spread.' Tilly clapped her paws at the thought of a Furcross tea, and suddenly felt a pang of hunger as the smell of freshly baked pies filled their room.

The telephone rang constantly for the rest of the morning and, by lunchtime, the No. 2 Feline Detective Agency was buzzing with possible cases and crank calls. Hettie and Tilly were so overwhelmed by their newfound popularity that they were forced to put the telephone back in the sideboard with a cushion on it for ten minutes to eat in peace. Tilly nipped to the Butters' shop to exchange their luncheon vouchers and received a hero's welcome from the queue, returning with two ham baps and a couple of 'not-quite-Cornish' pasties for their dinner. She found Hettie distraught after a particularly awkward caller had suggested that they may wish to dress up as chickens to solve a spate of golf buggy thefts from the local country club. The caller was clearly the worse for drink and, in the end, Hettie had told him so.

'So much for being on the front page of the *Sunday Bloody Snout*,' said Hettie, biting into her bap. 'The world's gone mad. Oh, and Hacky Redtop phoned back. He wants to do a "cases I have solved" feature.'

Tilly thought for a moment before offering her opinion. 'Well, that could prove a bit tricky. We could take on some of the easier cases, I suppose. The stake-outs could be fun as long as the weather's nice, but I don't suppose there will be many jobs as exciting as the Furcross case.'

When the ham baps had been dispatched, Tilly made some tea and Hettie glanced down the substantial list of possible cases that had come in that morning. 'The thing is, we need to choose jobs that require the least amount of effort for the most amount of money. Furcross was a one-off. I don't think anything like that will come along again. Most of the stuff here is just boring, and with the winter coming on we don't want to be stuck out in the cold shivering under lamp posts.'

Tilly nodded in agreement, thinking of how much worse her arthritis was in cold weather. 'What we need is a nice murder in a big house, with lots of servants who keep fires in every room and a big kitchen full of lovely food.'

Hettie scanned the list again. 'Well, there's nothing like that here. The most exciting prospect is Miss Spitforce's mysterious footprint. Maybe that will turn into a murder eventually.' The two cats laughed as a loud and urgent knock came at the door. Hettie sprang to answer it, having a very good idea of who it might be.

'Blimey!' said Poppa, struggling through the door with a huge box. 'Remind me not to do any more favours for Lazarus Hambone. He said it was a little delivery! I'll stick this here and go and fetch the other box from the van.' Poppa disappeared, and Hettie tried to contain her grin.

Tilly made her way round the box, sniffing and

patting it as if it had landed from Mars. 'Whatever is it?' she asked as she plucked up the courage to climb on top and remove the tape from the lid.

'Let's just call it a gift from a satisfied customer,' Hettie said, watching Poppa put another, smaller box down next to his bright orange toolkit.

Tilly was more puzzled than ever. 'But Marcia Woolcoat has already paid up. Why would she want to send anything else?'

'Who said it's from Marcia Woolcoat? This has come from another case altogether—a bit of spadework at Hambone's on Saturday afternoon to be exact.'

Poppa and Hettie burst out laughing, but Tilly failed to see the joke and jumped down feeling hurt and a little left out. Poppa reached into his overall pocket and pulled out some coins. 'I think this calls for cream horns all round while I unpack the boxes. Who's going to fetch them?' He looked straight at Tilly, who brightened and skipped off on her mission, leaving the contents of the two strange boxes to her friends.

The Butters' queue was a long one and, as it moved briskly forward, Tilly watched while the tray of cream horns gradually diminished. When her turn finally came there were only two left, and she was faced with a choice of custard doughnut or cream slice to make up the shortfall. Beryl—on counter duty—could see that Tilly was in two minds over her choice and put all four cakes into a bag, taking money for just three. They were the last cakes of the day, and Bery knew that if she and Betty were able to wipe down their surfaces with their usual efficiency, they could treat themselves to an hour at the local garden centre before it shut. Beryl grew vegetables and Betty flowers in the neat plot of land at the back of the bakery, and there were major decisions to be made regarding autumn planting. Anyway, an hour at the garden centre drinking tea and eating other people's cakes in the cafe was always a treat.

By the time Tilly returned with the cakes, the boxes had been unpacked and discarded in the yard. The cardboard flapped in the wind and threatened to take off as she came out of the passageway and headed for the back door. One of the boxes twisted round in a sudden gust to chase her, and Tilly dropped the cakes as she tried to fight off the attack. The giant wall of cardboard reared up in front of her and she grappled frantically with the door handle, and then—in an instant—the wind died. The cardboard collapsed and lay disinterested on the flagstones, and the cakes were rescued—no worse for being dropped in such an unceremonious fashion. Tilly progressed to the safety of their room, only to find Poppa and Hettie looking even more conspiratorial than they had when she left them.

She looked round and noticed that some of the

furniture had been moved. The staff sideboard was shoved along the wall closer to the door, and Hettie's armchair pointed in a slightly different direction, facing the corner of the room where a ghostly creature now stood, shrouded in Tilly's bed blanket.

'Just in time,' said Hettie, relieving Tilly of the bag of cakes. 'It's your surprise, so you can unveil it.'

Tilly looked from Hettie to Poppa and back again, hoping for a clue to what her blanket was hiding. As nothing was forthcoming, she moved towards the ghost in the corner, her heart still beating in her mouth from the cardboard incident in the yard. It was just as well that the Butters had chosen to go out: her squeal of sheer delight could easily have been misinterpreted as a murder being done on their premises; in fact, it probably reached as far down the High Street as Meridian Hambone herself, but Tilly was conscious only of the large television set and the strange-looking box that sat underneath it. As Poppa and Hettie prepared afternoon tea, she sat on her blanket in the middle of the floor and stared at the blank screen in front of her, hardly daring to take her eyes off it in case someone took it away again.

'Aren't you going to switch it on?' asked Hettie through a mouthful of cream cake. 'It won't bite.'

Tilly wasn't so sure about that. She got up and moved slowly towards the array of push-in silver buttons, locating the one that offered a choice of on or off. Carefully, she pressed it and closed her eyes, too excited to see what would happen next. The TV set sprang into life to reveal an episode of *Top Cat*, one of her all-time favourite cartoons. She opened one eye and then the other, putting her paws in her mouth to try and contain her excitement.

Poppa and Hettie were looking on, pleased, when the telephone began to ring to its merry, muffled self. 'That bloody phone hasn't stopped all day!' Hettie said, distracted. 'I wouldn't mind, but I'm a bit tired after all the Furcross and Malkin and Sprinkle stuff, not to mention fighting off Meridian Hambone's thugs.'

Satisfied at last that her surprise was going nowhere, Tilly joined them at the table just in time to get her paws around the custard doughnut. 'What exactly did happen in Hambone's?' she asked as Poppa put the kettle on for more tea. Hettie was about to recount the story when the TV switched itself off and the kettle died. 'Oh bugger! It's the electricity.' The three cats scrabbled around in their pockets for some change and Poppa finally came up with the right coins to feed the meter. Tilly slipped them happily into the slot, turning the key each time as the money clinked into the box. She loved putting coins in the meter; it reminded her of rare days out at the seaside when she and Hettie allowed themselves a few pennies for the slot machines. Last time, Tilly had managed three milk churns in a row and they had spent their winnings on fish and chips. This particular slot machine was a little more self-obsessed and swallowed everything she had. When the electricity surged once more through the room, Hettie treated Poppa and Tilly to a brave and noble version of what she now called the 'Hambone Case', then the three cats discussed the resurrection of Alma Mogadon and its possible implications for Furcross. With Tilly taking notes, Poppa then demonstrated the delights of video recording while Hettie eyed up the remaining cream slice. An uncharacteristic bout of self-control saved her waistline from any further damage, and by the time Poppa got up to leave, it had been decided that he should drop the cake off at Jessie's on his way home.

He gathered his tools together as the six o'clock news started and Oralia Claw's face flashed onto the screen. There was an interview with Mr Malkin and Mr Sprinkle, who both talked of Hettie's bravery and Jessie's 'have a go' spirit, and there were various comments from some of the fashion show models. Cocoa Repel was captured on film leaving her flat, but raised her paw in front of the cameras to stop them getting a close-up as she was driven off at high speed in a taxi. It seemed that it was going to take some time for the Furcross Case to die a natural death, and Hettie was beginning to understand the burden of celebrity; surprisingly, it didn't sit too well with her.

She walked Poppa to his long twin-wheel base transit, which was parked outside Oralia Claw's nail bar. 'I forgot to tell you,' he said, searching his pockets for the keys, 'those two villains you sorted in Hambone's—guess who they were?'

Hettie thought for a moment. 'I've no idea, although they did look familiar. Nasty pieces of work, both of them.'

'You're right there. They come from a whole family of crooks and murderers, and you had a narrow escape taking them on—even the gypsies will have nothing to do with them. Threw them out of the camp years ago along with their sister.'

'What's their sister got to do with it?'

'Everything,' replied Poppa with satisfaction. 'Their sister was Oralia Claw, and I'd put money on the Claw brothers being involved in taking the bodies from Furcross to help their little sister out.' He sped off down the High Street, leaving Hettie standing open-mouthed on the pavement.

CHAPTER SEVENTEEN

For a whole week, the High Street buzzed with talk of Oralia Claw's downfall and the scandal surrounding it. A 'To Let' sign went up outside the nail bar, and the occasional group of sightseers stopped to take photographs of the shopfront as a trophy of its notoriety. Tilly was mobbed by High Street gossips, out in full force for any extra tit-bits that could be spread further afield, and Jessie wore her cuts and bruises with pride as her little shop boomed with customers, all wanting to get a good look at her. She agreed with Tilly that her wrestling match with Oralia Claw had proved extremely lucrative in the scheme of things and, as an act of reparation, Cocoa Repel had donated several rails of her now-doomed collection to be sold in the designer section. Hettie had only to venture across the road to collect her savings book to receive an impromptu round of applause from Lavender Stamp's queue, which grew and grew like Topsy once word got out that Hettie had taken her place in it.

Mr Malkin and Mr Sprinkle sent a large hamper of food to the No. 2 Feline Detective Agency, with a 'thank you' note signed by both of them. It took Hettie and Tilly the best part of Friday to unpack it all, as they indulged themselves in the delights of daytime TV. Tilly had popped out to choose a video from Turner Page's library van, only to be driven back by an inquisition that wouldn't die down, and the telephone that never used to ring had been put out next to the Butters' ovens in disgrace—or, in Hettie's words, 'because it didn't know when to shut up'. Life was clearly not going to be the same, and Hettie and Tilly were doing their best to adjust to the fall-out of the Furcross Case, which had brought them riches as well as unlooked-for responsibilities. They had possible cases coming out of their ears, but neither of them had the heart or the inclination to follow them up. What had begun as an exciting foray into the art of detection had, in reality, turned out to be an insight into a world of obsessed, damaged, greedy cats, and—as far as Hettie could see—no real happy endings.

Saturday welcomed in a new month and, as if on cue, the October wind gathered in strength throughout the morning. Hettie grappled with the coal scuttle as Tilly—instinctively preparing for winter—washed and pegged out all their blankets, taking advantage of the drying weather. The Butters' small backyard opened out into a substantial plot with a path that ran its length, separating the vegetable garden from what Betty liked to call their 'sitting out patch'; this area was laid to lawn, with a host of plants and shrubs dotted about the borders. Having delivered the coal to its place by the fire, Hettie returned to the yard and made her way up the garden to the small shed which had been offered as her personal storage area; there, she kept the trappings of her many lives, all gathered together in haste when her shed-with-a-bed was taken in the great storm. She rarely visited her shed these days. There was very little she could identify with now that her life had taken on a normality which came with age and a greater need for comfort. But today she unlocked the padlock and gently pulled the door open, experiencing some resistance from hinges that had—like Hettie—become set in their ways.

Her time capsule was piled high with what on first inspection might seem of very little value to anyone seeking treasure. But treasure there was. The musician she had been sang loud and clear from the endless mounted posters, piled high on top of each other and showing a younger self. There were boxes of albums, all with her name stamped above the titles and offering various incarnations of her musical progression. Some had sold well; others had disappeared without a trace; but all were very much part of her journey through life. Hettie picked her way across the floor, catching the cobwebs with her paws as she went, searching in the gloom for something precious. Suddenly there it was, propped up on her old red bean bag, admittedly looking a little worse for wear but just as inviting as it had ever been: the twelve-string guitar had lain in wait for this moment and, in spite of its only possessing nine strings, Hettie embraced it. Slumping down on the bean bag, she began to tune the remaining rusty strings and tease a few random chord progressions from her old friend. She lost all track of time, and had revisited a number of her big numbers before noticing her audience. Tilly had slipped into the shed and was silently clapping her paws in appreciation of a rather lurid murder ballad. By the end of the sorry tale, she could no longer contain her delight at the impromptu performance and began to cheer, causing Hettie to break yet another string; it twanged across the shed, finally coming to rest on a full set of reindeer antlers that had been bestowed on her during her triumphant 'Arctic Circle' tour.

'Oh you did make me jump! How long have you been there?' Hettie asked, struggling to release herself from the bean bag.

'Long enough to know that your guitar ought to come and live with us rather than gathering dust in this shed. Some of these posters would cheer up our walls, too.' Tilly launched herself enthusiastically into the mountain of memorabilia, selecting a couple of colourful examples of Hettie caught on stage with her band. 'We'll ask Poppa to put them up for us next time he drops in. I think we could have a sort out in here—there's lots of nice things we could use.

That bean bag would make an extra chair, and the guitar could live on it when we're not using it.'

Before Hettie could argue, Tilly dragged the bean bag across the floor and loaded her selection of posters onto it. She disappeared down the garden path, leaving Hettie to lock up and carry her now eight-string guitar to the relative safety of their room. It had taken her some time to revisit a past she mourned, but it had only taken Tilly five minutes to reunite her with all that was good about herself.

With the chores out of the way and Hettie's guitar installed on its bean bag, their thoughts turned to a light lunch before afternoon tea at Furcross. There was no shopping to be done, as the contents of the Malkin and Sprinkle hamper would last them for some time, and at least that saved them from the prying eyes of weekend shoppers. She selected two tins of luxury sardines in extra tomato sauce from the hamper, and they settled to the task of opening them. Hettie's tin opened without incident but Tilly's key wouldn't turn more than halfway across, where it became stuck fast. 'Why do they make it so difficult to open sardines?' she asked, tugging at the key. 'The tomato sauce ends up spraying itself everywhere. They put pilchards in a proper tin so you can use a tin opener, so why can't they do the same with these?!' She was getting tearful with the frustration of being able to see her sardines but not eat them, and Hettie—sensing the approaching disaster—gave Tilly hers to eat while she took up the battle between key, fish, tin and more particularly tomato sauce. When the lid finally gave way, the sauce cascaded all over Tilly, Hettie and a sizeable area of their gingham tablecloth; in fact it was several months later, when Tilly had occasion to climb on top of the filing cabinet to change a light bulb, that she finally removed the last splashes of tomato from the ceiling.

'I think we might have to buy a car,' said Hettie, dabbing the sauce from her fur. 'We need to be able to get out and about under our own steam. Poppa has been wonderful, but he's a busy plumber and he isn't always available. I don't think we should be seen catching buses too often—it's not good for our image.' The fact that Tilly was still covered almost entirely in tomato sauce had given rise to thoughts on how they should project themselves; in Hettie's book, image was everything.

'Cars are very expensive,' Tilly said thoughtfully. 'They drink lots of petrol and the old ones are always stopping whenever they feel like it. Miss Lambert had one. It was green with real leather seats and she had to wind it up. It never started on frosty mornings and she usually had to push it home. I'm not sure we'd get on with a car.'

'But you don't have to wind them up any more,' Hettie argued in defence of the modern motor car. 'They almost drive themselves these days.'

'That's what I mean—they do as they like,' countered Tilly. 'What if we wanted to go to the seaside and IT wanted to go shopping? I bet IT would win. You're always hearing taxi drivers apologising for being late because they got lost. Well, that's what happens with cars: they make you late because they please themselves where they go and how long it takes them. And even if you do get somewhere in a car, where do you park it? Have you seen those meters on sticks? They're everywhere, and if you park by one of those you have to put money in it. Why would you want to do that? And if you don't put money in it, one of those nasty know-it-all cats with a peaked cap will give you a ticket for your trouble.'

Tilly cleared away the empty tins as Hettie, feeling a little defeated, glanced through the local advertiser, now also covered in sardines and tomato sauce. One advert leapt off the page at her. 'Well I never! Look at this! "RECONDITIONED MOTOR BIKES AND SIDECARS".' The ad went on to list a number of machines that were 'as good as new', finishing with a contact number and address, and it was that which made Hettie's heart sing: 'Enquiries c/o Hambone's Hardware.'

Forgetting her personal war with the motor car, Tilly bounced onto the table to read over Hettie's shoulder. 'Ooh! I wouldn't mind one of those. I once lived in a sidecar in a garage for three weeks until I was discovered and turned out. It was ever so cosy at night—just like having my own little place. Can we go and look at one?'

Hettie was pleased that Tilly wasn't averse to all modes of transport, and grew quite excited at the prospect of their detective agency having wheels. 'I'm not sure we can afford these prices, but the Hambones may be able to offer a good deal on one if we save up a bit. We could go and look at some on our way to Furcross to see if we like them, but you'll have to get cleaned up first. You look like something from a horror film with all that red sauce everywhere.'

Tilly sprang into action, filling their sink with soapy water and scrubbing away at her fur until all traces of lunch had been removed. Hettie did the same and ten minutes later they set out down the High Street. It was a week since Meridian Hambone had been set about by the Claw brothers and Hettie had come to her rescue, but life seemed to stand still in the dusty Aladdin's cave. Meridian sat as she always did, perched on her stool by the till and offering toothless grins as an introduction to her emporium of domestic delights. Seeing Hettie, she let out a squawk like an old crow. 'Gawd love us! If it ain't me guardian angel! What brings yer in today?'

Hettie stepped forward while Tilly hovered by the watering cans, wondering if Meridian stocked a special tin opener for sardines but was too frightened to ask. 'Well, I noticed an ad for motorbikes and sidecars in the paper and it said to contact Hambone's. I wondered if we could have a look at them?'

Meridian displayed her very best toothless grin. 'Them's Lazarus's. 'E does the bigger stuff in the yard out the back. 'E's out there now tunin' 'em up. You go through the shop and out the door by me 'lectrics.'

The backyard of Hambone's was a sight to behold. On first glance it was piled high with scrap metal, but a closer inspection revealed it to be the place where new life was given to old things. There was a small caravan over in the corner which, from the signage on its window, functioned as the sales office. Hettie could see Lazarus Hambone inside with another cat and, as she and Tilly approached, he emerged with his customer, counting a wad of notes to conclude a deal. The customer left through a pair of double gates at the back of the yard and Lazarus shut them firmly behind him before returning to the office. 'Miss Bagshot—I wasn't expectin' royalty today! What can I do fer the most famous cat in town? 'Cept fer Oralia Claw, that is.'

Hettie's ears blushed at his words and Tilly— believing that Lazarus Hambone really was a giant—hid behind her. 'We've come to see if you have a motorbike and sidecar that we could run about in,' Hettie said. 'We think it would help if we had some transport for our detective agency.'

Lazarus beamed, showing a full set of pearly white teeth that had obviously not been inherited from his mother. 'I got just the thing! Perfect for a couple of go-getters like yerselves. Follow me.' He led them past a mountain of exhaust pipes, old tyres and bits of engine to an area roped off from the yard's general chaos—and there stood two neat rows of motorbikes and sidecars. They were all in various states of renovation: some waiting for handlebars, others undergoing complete paint jobs, and one looking ready and willing to take to the road. 'This one's a good'un. She's got a few 'undred miles left in 'er, ideal for a first go, an' the sidecar's got plenty of room. Nice little runner altogether. I can just picture you two solvin' yer crimes in this.'

Tilly was impressed. She circled the machine, giving out little murmurs of appreciation as she admired the contrast of the shiny black mudguards against the bright red body of the sidecar, then marvelled at the bike's highly polished chrome and her own satisfied reflection in it. Hettie stood back and watched, too frightened to go anywhere near a thing of such beauty which she knew they could never afford. Her disappointment grew as Lazarus—seeing that Tilly was well and truly hooked—moved to pull back the lid on the sidecar as the final clincher on the deal. 'This is far too grand for us, Mr Hambone,' she said hurriedly.

'Do you have anything a little more . . . er . . . rough and ready?' She saw Tilly's face fall but knew that the only sensible thing to do was to bring the dream to an end before the interior of the sidecar was revealed.

Lazarus Hambone had been selling motorbikes long enough to know that 'no' usually meant 'yes' with a little extra push here and there. He would always be grateful to Hettie for saving his mother from the Claw brothers, and it was time to put his bargaining skills to work. 'I tell yer what I'll do. I'll take yer out for a spin on 'er, so's you can get the feel of it, and if yer still likes what yer see, I'll work out a plan so's yer can pay me a bit at a time. I'm not in any hurry for the money and I can offer yer a very good price. I owes yer, and a Hambone always settles 'is debts.'

Tilly, who had placed herself between Hettie and the giant Lazarus, stared from one to the other, waiting and hoping that they would soon be heading out onto the open road in the shiny red creature that had stolen her heart. Hettie looked into Lazarus's face and saw an honesty she didn't expect from a wheeler and dealer. Without any further conversation, she nodded and turned towards the motorbike. Lazarus slid back the lid on the sidecar and Tilly—using one of the shiny black mudgards as a step—leapt into the seat which offered space for two. When he returned from his caravan with helmet and goggles, he found both cats sitting in the sidecar, excitedly waiting for their ride. 'I brought you an extra pair of goggles in case yer wants to ride pillion,' he said, seeing how comfortable Hettie and Tilly had made themselves in their little red bubble.

Hettie hadn't had time to consider that she would eventually have to master the motorbike, and was quite content to sit with Tilly in the comfort of the sidecar while Lazarus Hambone put the vehicle through its paces. 'I'm happy just to watch from here at the moment, Mr Hambone,' she said. 'And anyway, I'm wearing my very best mac. I think I'll need something a little more practical if I'm to ride astride.' Tilly giggled at Hettie's motorbike talk, and knew that she could soon start to plan an interior revamp for the sidecar destined to become an important part of the No. 2 Feline Detective Agency.

Lazarus wheeled them out onto the road, shutting the double gates behind him, then leapt onto the motorbike and kicked it into life. With a roar, they shot off down the road, turned right into the High Street, and sped away through the outskirts of the town and out into the countryside. Hettie and Tilly clung to each other in sheer delight and shouted above the noise of the motorbike. 'It's just like a ride at the fair!' screamed Tilly, as Lazarus swung round a corner. 'We're going to have such fun! We could even go to the seaside in it.'

Hettie looked up at the giant, be-goggled form

211

of Lazarus Hambone as he gave the motorbike its full throttle and wondered how long it would take her to master the art of being a biker—but that problem was for another day. 'I think we'll have to buy it, whatever it costs,' she shouted to Tilly, as main roads gave way to winding lanes lined with the colours of autumn.

The deal was done by the time Lazarus dropped them at the entrance to Furcross. Hettie had been offered terms that she simply could not refuse, and Lazarus had also promised to teach her the basics of the road. He expected this aspect of the deal to take some time, and so it was agreed that Hettie would present herself at his yard every Tuesday tea time for the foreseeable future until she had got the hang of it. Tilly put herself forward as added support; the idea of being driven around country lanes in the bright red sidecar appealed to her almost as much as watching TV and—as their new mode of transport was to be kept in Hambone's yard until Hettie was capable of driving it away—it would be her only chance to see it.

They waved Lazarus off and headed for the front door of Furcross, which was flung open long before they had even thought of knocking. Marcia Woolcoat stood on the threshold, bedecked in what could easily have been a bright orange tent had it not chosen to feature a double row of large lime green buttons down its front. 'Miss Bagshot! How splendid of you and your friend to honour us with your presence! Please come through to my parlour, where Marley is about to serve tea.'

By now, Hettie was more than used to Marcia Woolcoat's fluctuating moods, but this welcome was over the top even by her standards. Feeling a little nervous, she hung her designer mac on her usual peg and followed the matron of Furcross down the corridor, with Tilly skipping along behind, straightening her best red cardigan as she went.

Marcia Woolcoat's parlour had transformed itself into a warm, vibrant haven of colour. There was a blazing fire in the grate, the photographs had returned to the walls and mantelpiece, and several vases of chrysanthemums stood around the room in autumn shades of gold and red. The sofa that had so often been the battleground for Marcia Woolcoat's inner demons was now occupied by a very pretty cat dressed in a blue jumper and matching trousers, with a cheerful spotted scarf around her neck. Hettie had to look at her twice to work out who she was; after all, dead cats look very different to live ones, as she remarked to Tilly later.

'Please sit down Miss Bagshot, and your friend? Miss . . . er . . . ?'

'This is Tilly, just Tilly, and I would prefer to be called Hettie instead of Miss Bagshot,' Hettie said, squashing herself onto the sofa next to Tilly and Alma Mogadon. 'It seems much friendlier.'

'Oh, I'm so pleased. In that case, you may call

me Marcia and my sister here is Alma. I feel we have known each other for years, Miss . . . er . . . Hettie, and I hope our friendship will endure. How can I ever thank you for restoring my sister to me and making me see the error of my ways?' Marcia batted a tear away with her paw and sat down in her armchair opposite the sofa, addressing her remarks to all three cats. 'Before Marley gets here with the tea, there are a number of things I wish to say. My sister and I have spent the week laying ghosts to rest and talking about our future, which we are very much looking forward to—but before we can embrace what is to come, I must put things right and remember whom I have to thank for pulling the scales from my eyes.' Hettie, Tilly and Alma all leant forward, completely transfixed as Marcia Woolcoat continued. 'When I first invited my sister to join me at Furcross, it was more from my need for a qualified nurse than a wish to indulge a family member, but, as time went on, Alma became the sister I thought I had lost. As you now know, I have been estranged from my mother for many years. She made it clear when Alma was born that she didn't want me in her life, and I endured some terrible acts of cruelty before I decided to make my own way in the world. I missed my sister when I left, but I vowed to myself that I wouldn't return, even if it meant never seeing Alma again. My mother found it impossible to love us both, and she had made

214

her choice. By the time Alma and I were reunited at Furcross, our mother had become a difficult and demanding elderly cat, and—having lavished so much love on Alma—she fully expected that my sister would look after her in her later years. I refused to take any part in this problem, and made Alma choose between us. I now realise that this was an impossible position in which to put my sister. My lack of understanding nearly cost Alma her life, and if it hadn't been for you and your careful handling of the case on which I engaged you, I fear there would have been a very different outcome.'

As Marcia's last remark was addressed directly at Hettie, she had no alternative but to allow her ears to blush a bright red. Tilly fidgeted on her behalf, sharing a nod of approval with Alma, who seemed to be hanging on Marcia's every word. And the words continued. 'I am fully aware of the outcome regarding Oralia Claw and the deception in which she encouraged my sister to take part, but I am most grateful that you have resisted revealing the full story to the papers and have somehow managed to keep Alma and Furcross out of the news. It is to your credit that you go about your business in such a way that the innocent are protected and the guilty are brought to book— but I am also guilty, which is why I feel the need to confess and make reparation to those I have hurt.'

There was an almighty crash as Marley Toke

fell into the room, pushing a tea trolley laden with cakes and sandwiches and almost unseating the samovar. 'Oh my days, Miss Marcie! Me trolley's lost a wheel. Dat lurched out o' me grasp on de way from me kitchen, and it took me all me time to catch it. Den, just as me get 'ere, de front wheel go somewhere else!' Tilly and Alma sprang to Marley's rescue, steadying the trolley as the cook selected one of Digger Patch's novels from the shelf and shoved it under the offending corner. Tilly couldn't help but remember that the last time she and the trolley had been in such close contact there was a dead cat on the bottom shelf, but she was pleased to see that it was now taken up with the most delicious of teatime treats: fish paste sandwiches with the crusts cut off; small pork pies; cheese straws; crisps; a huge chocolate cake; and a mountain of iced buns in pink, lemon and white.

Marcia seemed to have lost the thread of what she was about to say, much to the relief of Alma, Hettie and Tilly, who now gathered round Marley's trolley as she poured tea from the samovar and handed it out. The plates were distributed and piled high with sandwiches and, for the next ten minutes, the only sound in Marcia Woolcoat's parlour was a contented, rhythmic chewing and the smacking of lips. When the sandwiches had been disposed of, Marcia led the way with the cheese straws and pork pies, and Marley—having joined in with the savouries—

216

prepared to cut the chocolate cake, which no doubt had Jamaican origins.

The cake was a huge success and a party atmosphere took over the small parlour. Tilly had made a firm friend of Alma, who seemed to like all the books and films that numbered among Tilly's favourites, and who—most importantly— was the proud owner of Elizabeth Traybake's autograph, which she had got on a train before the actress moved to Hollywood. Hettie helped Marley to load the empty cups and plates back onto the trolley, and Marcia Woolcoat—having eaten and drunk everything within reach— resumed her presentation. The gathered few settled themselves back on the sofa with the exception of Marley, who—without invitation— flopped down on the rug by the fire.

Seeing that she once again commanded their attention, Marcia continued. 'I have come to a number of decisions regarding the future of Furcross, and my sister and I have decided to embark on a fresh enterprise in pastures new.'

'Oh Miss Marcie, what will I do?!' wailed Marley, covering her face with her apron as her substantial body rose and fell in giant sobs.

Marcia Woolcoat was horrified at her reaction, and quickly addressed the situation. 'Marley— please let me finish. I am very aware of your loyalty both to me and to Alma during your time here, and for that reason I have decided to take on the lease of Oralia Claw's premises in the hope that you will consider running a cafe of your own in the High Street.' Marley allowed the apron to drop from her eyes and sat open-mouthed. 'My sister and I are happy to invest in your skills and, in exchange for your managing the day-to-day running of the venture, we would be happy to offer you a partnership and a good share of the profits. There is, I believe, living accommodation above the shop which should, in time, make a comfortable home for you. How does that sound?'

It was some time before Marley could find any words and all eyes turned in her direction, anticipating her response; when it came, it was worth waiting for. 'Is you sayin' dat you givin' me a cookin' shop? And dat you puttin' me in charge? And dat I'll have me own place, a proper home where day can say—Marley Toke, she live 'ere? Oh Miss Marcie! Dat sound de best ting dat ever happened to me in all me days.'

'Yes Marley, that's exactly what I am saying. You will obviously have to work hard to make it a success, but Alma and I think you can do it and we are both happy to help in any way we can. I have arranged with the agents to collect the keys on Monday, after they have cleared the place of Oralia Claw's things. I suggest you go and have a look at the property and start making plans as soon as you can.'

Marley pulled herself up with the aid of the mantelpiece and threw herself into her benefactor's arms as the sobs returned, this time of sheer joy. Bouncing off a startled Marcia, who had never learnt to hug anyone in her life, she repeated her show of gratitude on Alma, flattening her slight form against the arm of the sofa. Hettie and Tilly looked on with satisfaction, but both were curious as to what would happen to Furcross. It hadn't occurred to Marley to ask, and so Hettie did the job for her. 'Where will you and Alma go? And what will happen to your guests here at Furcross?'

Marcia Woolcoat paused before answering Hettie's question, as if waiting for Alma to speak, but her sister just smiled and nodded, encouraging Marcia to outline their plans. 'Due to the recent problems here, most of our guests have left and those who remain are happy to make alternative plans. Miss Ledge has accepted a proposal from Mr Slack and it is their intention to purchase a cottage in the country. Miss Marilyn Repel has received some very exciting news from a film company in Hollywood. I understand that she is being offered a contract to become the senior lead in a high-profile TV series entitled *Desperate Housecats*. She has managed to procure a wardrobe contract for her daughter Cocoa, who under the . . . er . . . circumstances is happy to leave these shores for a new life in Hollywood. As for Furcross, I had a most satisfactory meeting with Mr Turner Page earlier today. He is keen to reinstate the town's library and feels that Furcross would be an ideal building. The new venture would also include a day centre for elderly cats and a nursery for young kittens. As a condition of purchase, he has agreed to turn the burial ground into a memorial garden where cats can buy their own plots.' Realising that she was headed for murky waters, Marcia shot a look at Alma and moved on. 'There will of course be no facilities for our Dignicat programme, but it's good to know that the residents who already have their resting places in the burial ground will lie undisturbed.'

Hettie suddenly recalled with great clarity her zombie dream and wondered whether it was Turner Page who would be disturbed by the burial ground's permanent residents rather than the other way round. Choosing to keep her macabre thoughts to herself, she pressed Marcia into revealing hers and Alma's future plans. This time, Alma readily took up the baton.

'Marcia has spoken of her guilt and of how she wishes to make reparation, but it is my confession that you must hear. The fault lies with me. As you are all aware, my mother has expressed a wish to spend her final years by the sea, and it was my efforts to make this happen without Marcia's knowledge that led to the terrible mess I found myself in and the awful things I allowed to happen to Pansy, Vita and Virginia. I involved my best friend Marley in my secrets, and worst of all I put my sister through the most painful of situations, first by attempting to take my own life and then by allowing her to discover my deceit regarding our mother. The best thing to come out of this mess is that there are now no secrets, and I have you all to thank for that. The days I spent in my room, hovering between life and death, believing that I had died and was spending my afterlife imprisoned in a tomb of my own making, have taught me that nothing is so bad that it can't be talked about. That's what Marcia and I have been doing all this week.' Marcia reached out and took her sister's paw, and Alma continued. 'My mother is a difficult cat and can be very cruel and spiteful, but she *is* my mother and I couldn't just walk away from my responsibilities when she has always loved me. I didn't want to choose between her and my sister. I know that Marcia has every good reason not to see my mother again, but she is old and needs looking after.'

Hettie was beginning to tire of the Marcia and Alma confessional; in fact, they were both getting on her nerves. Tilly obviously felt the same way, because she was fidgeting and picking threads out of Marcia Woolcoat's sofa. The idea of a fire in their own grate and a choice of Saturday night viewing on their TV had far greater appeal than the humble pie which was being consumed in front of them, but the problem was how to extricate themselves from the situation without causing offence.

It was Marley who came to the rescue. 'Lord love us, Moggy girl! Don't put yourself through all dat trouble again. Just tell us what you and Miss Marcie doin' next.'

Alma brightened at the prospect of talking about the future but the opportunity was snatched from her by Marcia Woolcoat. 'We have decided to buy a big house by the sea—in Southwool if we can find one—and when we are settled our mother will come to live with us on the understanding that she has separate accommodation and that Alma takes complete control of her.'

Hettie noticed the word 'control' as opposed to 'care' and wondered how their mother would take to living under a regime designed by Marcia Woolcoat; maybe it was payback time for all of them. Tilly was trying to imagine what Marcia's and Alma's mother looked like; the colour combination of ginger, pink and grey with a mix of short and long hair and an aptitude for drama which she had clearly passed to her offspring gave a rather unpleasant picture. Hopefully she would never have to find out.

Marcia and Alma seemed to have run out of steam, and Hettie chose exactly the right moment to stand up. Tilly followed her example, brushing chocolate cake crumbs from the front of her cardigan, and Hettie gave their thanks for tea and what had turned out to be two hours of enlightenment. They moved towards the door, politely waiting for someone to see them out.

Alma stood as if to follow them but made for the tea trolley instead. Taking the cake slice, she cut another large piece of chocolate cake and took it to Marcia, who waved it away. 'Oh come on, Marcia,' she said. 'You always were a greedy girl, and judging by the size of you nothing has changed. Surely you can manage another slice while I tell our guests what you're really like?' Everyone in the room froze except Alma, who placed the unwanted cake in Marcia's lap and moved to the fireplace, resting the cake slice carefully on the mantelpiece. 'As my sister has chosen to make our private family business so public, I think it only fair to come clean on her behalf—she seems unable to cope with the truth of any sort, especially concerning herself. You have heard a credible, heartwarming confession of her guilt which was worthy of an amateur stage production, and I have also played my part as any devoted sister should. But now we turn to the real Marcia Woolcoat.'

Marcia pushed herself out of her chair, letting the cake fall to the floor, but Alma was too quick for her and forced her back. 'Oh no you don't! This time you will let *me* speak, without interruption. It would be quite wrong to let our friends leave with a false impression, wouldn't it, sister dear?' Alma spat the last words out and Hettie and Marley exchanged worried looks. Tilly shrank behind

Hettie, still listening but not wanting to see what happened next. Marcia Woolcoat sat deflated and frightened as Alma continued. 'Last week, thinking I was dead, my sister carried me to my room and sat at my bedside for the first night—not out of remorse or grief, you understand, but out of her own selfish need to confess a crime she had committed many years ago. I was aware of her and could hear what she was saying, but the paralysis caused by the drug I had taken gave no indication of this and Marcia believed she was talking to a corpse. She spoke of her hatred for my mother and how she had been beaten, locked up and starved by her when I was a small kitten. But then the real truth came out.' Marcia gave a sob and started to shake, but Alma ignored her and carried on with her story. 'She said she had despised my mother for wanting more kittens, and that when I was born there was also another kitten—my twin sister, whom my mother had named Buffy. Marcia said that after our birth my mother was unwell and relied on her to take care of us. I have no memory of this time but, as I lay in a coma, my sister confessed that she had tried several times to kill me and Buffy, and eventually got half lucky. She told me that she had taken us down to the river, tied us up in a sack and thrown us both into the water. A neighbour watched her do it and pulled the sack out, but it was too late for Buffy. She died on the riverbank. Marcia ran away but my mother found her and brought her home, where she was locked up as a punishment and kept away from me in case she tried to finish the job. My mother never told me why she had taken against Marcia, but I can easily understand now her reasons for keeping me so close and for shutting Marcia out of her life as soon as she was old enough to make her own way in the world. In short, my sister destroyed my mother's life and nearly succeeded in doing the same to me. As for Buffy, she was given no life at all.'

Marcia Woolcoat forced herself out of her chair and this time turned on Alma. 'I have spent this week trying to make up for all that! I have even put Furcross in both our names so that we're equal, and I am willing to allow that cat you call a mother to shelter under my roof. I was very young and very jealous when I did what I did, and I suffered for it. When I thought you had killed yourself because of me, I had to confess. What more do you want from me?'

Alma smiled at Marcia as she took the cake slice from the mantelpiece and thrust it into her sister's stomach. 'Justice for Buffy and my mother, that's what I want.'

Marcia Woolcoat fell forward as a fountain of blood sprayed the room. No one could quite remember what happened next, but Marcia was clearly beyond help and it was some time before anyone moved. Still smiling, Alma Mogadon rescued the chocolate cake from the floor and began to eat it. It was Marley Toke who eventually took control of the situation, throwing a rug over the body that lay in a pool of blood by the fire. She reached out to Alma, who seemed oblivious to anything but the cake, and said: 'Come on now, Moggy—time for a lie-down. Me take you to yer room, then Marley she clean up and make Miss Marcie comfortable.' She steered Alma to the door and Hettie opened it for them, watching as Marley led Alma Mogadon down the corridor towards the hospital block. Shocked and silent, Hettie and Tilly made their way to the front door where Hettie collected her mac, and emerged into fresh air, glad to leave the Furcross bloodbath behind.

Neither of them spoke until they reached the bus stop in Sheba Gardens. 'It's just like that film,' Tilly said. 'You know the one—*Whatever Happened to Kitty Jane?* That was about two sisters—one was spiteful and the other was nasty. It starred . . . now let me think . . . er . . . was it Joan Clawfoot and Butty Daydream?'

Hettie thought for a moment as the bus loomed into view. 'Yes, I think you're right, but being stabbed by your own cake slice takes some beating, even in Hollywood. I think *Psycho* would be nearer the mark. I wonder if the old mother cat has a rocking chair and wears a wig?' Tilly wanted to giggle, but for some reason found that she couldn't.

CHAPTER EIGHTEEN

Marcia Woolcoat's funeral was set for the following Friday. The townsfolk had been saddened by her untimely and unfortunate death, and Hacky Redtop had written a very nice piece in the paper about her valued place in the community and her determination to offer a decent life to elderly cats at Furcross. Her death had been reported as a terrible accident: she had, according to the newspaper, slipped on a piece of chocolate cake and fallen on the point of her cake slice during a tea party attended by her now grieving sister and other unnamed friends. The funeral service and burial were to be held at Furcross, and the Thursday edition of the evening paper carried an open invitation from the family of the deceased, stating that all would be welcome to the interment and the wake that followed.

Hettie, Tilly and Poppa arrived in plenty of time, which was just as well; judging by the cars that were double-parked the length of Sheba Gardens, the whole of the town had turned out to pay its respects. Hettie and Tilly were suitably attired in their best macs with collars turned up against the October winds, and Poppa had exchanged his work overalls for a smart double-breasted seaman's jacket with shiny silver buttons. Marley, wearing some sort of tribal sarong, stood at the front door and greeted the mourners as they arrived, directing them through to the dining room where Marcia Woolcoat's open casket stood on trestles for final farewells.

Hettie and Tilly had pondered the passing of Marcia Woolcoat for most of that week and had eventually come to the conclusion that it was one of those messes that families got themselves into. There was no right or wrong involved, and it certainly wasn't their business to contradict the accepted version of Marcia Woolcoat's 'fatal accident'. Anyway, as Hettie had pointed out that morning: 'If we're going to be proper detectives, we can't afford to become emotionally involved with the personal lives of our clients.'

Tilly spotted Jessie in the crush of cats filling the dining room and made her way across to her. 'I was hoping I'd see you here, but I wasn't sure if you'd come.'

'I wouldn't have missed it for the world,' said Jessie, adjusting the red hat that had been knocked sideways by a tall cat's elbow. 'Marley called me in to dress her,' she added, nodding towards the casket. 'And it was no mean feat. I'd say that if the cake slice hadn't finished her, the cake would have done it. I managed to squeeze her into one of Cocoa's latest creations, but it's not done up at the back. Unless she surprises us by sitting up in her coffin, all should be well. Come and see what you think.'

Jessie and Tilly joined Poppa and Hettie by the casket, and all four cats looked for the last time on the face of Marcia Woolcoat. In death, as in life, she was a commanding figure, but no longer a threat. Hettie looked at her lifeless features and realised what a leveller death really was. She had become almost fond of Miss Woolcoat in a strange sort of way, but she could be fearsome and patronising and that part of her character had been her undoing. She had used her sister to hit back at her mother and manipulated the residents of Furcross into thinking her a saint, and now the whole town was buying into her benevolence by needing to be seen at her funeral. But Marcia must have waited in fear all her life for the justice that had finally come to her. Now, lying in her coffin like all the cats that had gone before, she would be nothing more than a few words on a headstone. Saddened, Hettie moved away from the main attraction as more cats jostled to see the corpse. She scanned the room for Alma Mogadon, but there was no sign of her.

The spectacle of Marcia Woolcoat's body was eventually eclipsed by the arrival of Marilyn Repel and her daughter Cocoa, who entered the dining room together wearing stunning full-length black dresses, finished off with shawls and studded with shiny black sequins and bugle

229

beads; both wore small skullcaps and delicate nets, pulled down low over their faces. Marley Toke left her post and, with the help of Turner Page, handed out small glasses of sherry to those seeking refreshment. Lavender Stamp, who had arrived earlier with the Butters, made a beeline for the tray of drinks and Hettie watched as she downed two glasses and took a third, which she carried across to Marcia's casket and sipped with appreciation as she looked the corpse up and down. There was still no sign of Alma Mogadon and Hettie was about to ask Marley where she was, when the French windows to the garden were flung open and four suited and booted cats moved swiftly through the crowd towards Marcia's coffin. One of them wielded a screwdriver, and the room fell silent as the lid to Miss Woolcoat's eternal overcoat was fixed in place and screwed down. The cats then positioned themselves, two either side of the coffin, and— with an act of herculean strength—hoisted the casket onto their shoulders on the count of three. The crowd held its breath as the undertakers reversed and turned the coffin; then, marching as one towards the French windows, they bore Marcia Woolcoat paws-first out of Furcross for the last time.

Her final journey across the lawn, past the potting shed and into the burial ground, was made a little more complicated by the gale force wind that erupted from nowhere, buffeting the coffin as the bearers struggled to maintain the dignity of the occasion. The mourners followed behind, hanging on to their hats, some arm in arm against the elements, and Hettie joined Tilly, Jessie and Poppa at the back of the procession; all had decided that they would get a much better view of the event by keeping their distance. By the time they arrived in the burial ground, a carnival atmosphere was developing, encouraged by the large, open-sided, red-and-white striped gazebo that had been erected next to the freshly dug grave. Marcia's plot had taken centre stage, and would no doubt become the focal point of the proposed memorial garden if the plan went ahead.

'What the hell is that?' asked Poppa, voicing his companions' concern.

'It looks like some sort of performance tent,' Hettie said, as the gazebo threatened to take off in another sudden gust of wind.

'The whole thing's a bit of a bloody performance if you ask me,' muttered Poppa, pulling his collar up against the first spots of rain.

Tilly was trying hard to see what was happening. Not sharing the same height as her friends, she eventually borrowed an abandoned flowerpot from the vegetable plot to stand on. 'Ah, that's better. Oh look! There's Alma in the tent, next to Marley. She seems to be smiling. Oh. Now she's laughing!'

Hettie and Jessie craned their necks as Poppa scrambled three more flowerpots from the garden, turning them upside down so that they could all get a decent view of the proceedings. In her new elevated position, Hettie had an excellent vantage point on the gazebo and was just in time to see Nola Ledge step inside to give the first reading. The wind carried her words away, but they must have been entertaining as Alma Mogadon continued to laugh; in fact, Hettie and Tilly noticed that Alma Mogadon smiled and laughed her way through the whole funeral, which was more than a little unsettling.

Next came Captain Silas Mariner, who produced a tin whistle and offered a jolly set of hornpipes to the wind and rain. Those who were not elite enough to come under the protection of the gazebo raised their umbrellas, much to Tilly's annoyance. 'Oh bugger! Now I can't see anything! Let's shove our way to the front—we're missing all the best bits.'

Tilly was right: the best bit was still to come. Poppa forced a path through the mourners and established a ringside position, and Jessie pushed her large red umbrella skyward to protect them all from the strengthening rain, bringing a bit of colour to an otherwise drab gathering. Marcia Woolcoat's coffin rested on planks across the open grave, and the rain danced and splashed off the lid as if joining in with one of Mariner's hornpipes. The music was brought to an abrupt end as the heavens opened wider in a violent downpour, and the undertakers responded by hurriedly tying ropes to the casket. With little further ceremony, they released the planks and lowered the coffin into the grave, which was rapidly filling with rainwater. Hettie couldn't help but remember the moment when Marcia Woolcoat had crawled out of a grave in the burial ground; now, that moment seemed like a macabre rehearsal, but she would need a good screwdriver to repeat the trick and pull off the resurrection that Hettie's imagination had created.

As the coffin was lowered, a number of mourners made their way back to the dining room out of the rain, ready to make inroads into the funeral tea that Marley had been up half the night preparing. But the show was by no means over: the rain eased and gave way to a sudden burst of sunshine, and the burial ground lit up and sparkled as the sun turned the raindrops into jewels of light. And out of that light came an everlasting promise of life after death.

'Oh my God!' exclaimed Hettie, looking across at the gazebo. 'It's Marcia Woolcoat! She's not dead! How has she done that? They've only just put her into her grave.' Hettie's outburst was heard by the remaining mourners, and all eyes turned towards the gazebo as Marcia Woolcoat stepped forward to address the crowd, bringing a smiling

Alma Mogadon with her. More discreetly this time, Hettie continued her commentary as Jessie, Poppa and Tilly stared open-mouthed. 'She's only going to take a bloody bow! No wonder Alma's laughing—it's all been a sick joke. That family obviously takes pride in coming back from the dead!'

Tilly could see that Hettie was getting angry and placed a paw on her arm, concerned that she may go too far. Marcia Woolcoat began to speak. 'Today is a celebration of life, the life of my dear daughter, Marcia.' Relieved, Hettie rallied. Marcia Woolcoat had been the spitting image of her mother, who now stood before them. It had never occurred to her that 'the old mother cat' was not quite as old as she had been painted, or that Marcia Woolcoat wasn't quite as young as she wished people to believe. Mrs Woolcoat senior continued. 'My beloved daughter wanted nothing more than to help those in need, and her work here at Furcross has made a real difference to so many lives. She cared for those who wanted dignity during their final days, and used her vast resources to that end. When my daughter Alma joined her here at Furcross, they made a wonderful team and I am so proud of them bot . And Marcia's work will continue: this place will be a shrine to her achievements thanks to a handsome offer from Mr Turner Page, who intends to bring community activities and a library service to the town. It is his wish that Furcross should be known from this day forward as the Marcia Woolcoat Community Centre and Memorial Garden.' The crowd cheered as Marcia Woolcoat's mother bathed herself in her daughter's legacy. When the appreciation had died down, she clapped her paws together in a triumphant gesture. 'And now let us all go back inside for a jolly good tea!'

The mood in the dining room was indeed a celebratory one. Marilyn Repel once again— and for the last time—offered her cabaret as the guests mingled, devouring vast quantities of food and drink. Hettie was still disturbed by the uncanny likeness of Marcia Woolcoat's mother, and was more than a little bewildered by her graveside speech; from what she had come to believe about the mother and daughter relationship, Marcia would be spinning in her grave and was likely to put in an appearance before her wake was over. The last few weeks had shown that stranger things really did happen.

Marley Toke had finally collapsed in a corner, exhausted but satisfied that the matron of Furcross had been given a send-off fit for royalty. Hettie joined her as many of the mourners began to say goodbye and head for their cars. 'What will you do now that Furcross is being taken over? Will you go ahead with the cafe?'

Marley looked thoughtful as she stared across the room at Alma Mogadon and her mother. 'De

235

ting is Miss Hettie—Moggy, she needs me. Just look at 'er—she bin grinnin' like dat since Miss Marcie's "accident", and de old mother cat, she want me to house keep for dem. Dey goin' to get a big house by de sea and dat would suit me very well. Me's not as young as me used to be, and startin' a cafe is a lot o' work.' Hettie nodded in agreement as Tilly joined them, carrying three large pieces of chocolate cake. 'You takes dat home, Miss Tilly. Me's gone off de chocolate cake just now.' Tilly realised her mistake and pushed the food to one side. Marley rose from her seat. 'I'll come and say me goodbyes in a day or two. Just now me has to 'arvest me plants from de yard before de Turner Page cat tinks they fixtures and fittings. I'll bring you some to dry for de winter. Dere's good pipe-smokin' catnip in dem plants.'

As Marley walked away across the dining room, Hettie noticed that Alma and her mother had stepped outside and were in conversation by the French windows. Curious and still a little confused by the day's events, she signalled to Tilly and they made their way towards the doors, positioning themselves within earshot of Marcia Woolcoat's mother as she shared a few thoughts with her only surviving daughter. 'You'll have to snap out of this, Alma! Take that stupid grin off your face or mummy is going to get very cross with you and have you locked away for good. Now we have her money, we can do anything we like. I told you that if we bided our time we'd get her in the end, and your nice little touch with the cake slice was brilliant. Now she's dead and we're rich, so pull yourself together! No more Marcia, no more Furcross. Just you and me and all that money.'

Alma remained silent throughout the one-sided conversation, but Hettie and Tilly moved forward as one when they heard her burst into a bout of convulsive laughter. The scissors appeared from nowhere and it was Tilly's swift action that saved the day: as Alma Mogadon raised her paw to strike, Tilly sprang through the French windows and pushed Mrs Woolcoat to the ground. The scissors missed their target and became firmly lodged in the nearest window box. Hettie grabbed Alma, restraining her as she hissed and spat at her mother. She tried to lead her back into the dining room, out of harm's way, but Alma resisted. 'How dare you threaten to have me locked up after everything you've put me through?' she shouted, glaring at the older cat who was struggling to regain her composure. 'I nearly died for you. I've cried myself to sleep at night worrying about you. I put up with Marcia's rules and regulations for you. I even killed her for you, and now you want to take her money and run my life with it? No, mother— your game is over. Marcia left all her money to *me,* and I'm sure she wouldn't have wanted me to share any of it with you, so unless you want me to finish what I started here, you will leave Furcross now and never try to contact me again.' Alma Mogadon turned away from her mother and headed across the lawn towards the burial ground. Shocked and defeated, Mrs Woolcoat walked slowly through the dining room and out into a world of loneliness, poverty and regret.

Tilly went to find Marley, knowing that Alma needed a friend to keep an eye on her, and Hettie followed the former nurse at a discreet distance, making sure that there were no further dramas to come. Alma stood by her sister's grave and sobbed for several minutes, then—realising she wasn't alone—turned to Hettie, her eyes still full of tears. 'I don't know what's happened to me,' she admitted quietly. 'It all got too much, being caught between my mother and my sister, and used by them both. I thought I loved my mother but I know now that I just felt sorry for her. As for Marcia, it was her guilt that brought us together— she wanted to make up for what she did to Buffy.' The tears came again and Alma's whole body shook as the years of pain and deceit engulfed her. Hettie found it difficult to watch as her features were twisted and distorted by anguish and sorrow, and she moved closer to help as Alma fell in front of Marcia's grave and cried to the heavens: 'Forgive me!'

The heavens responded with a deluge. Hettie made her move and gathered up what was left of Alma Mogadon, guiding her across the lawn and back into the dining room. The rain seemed to bring her to her senses: as Marley took charge of her friend and led her away, Alma turned back to Tilly and Hettie. 'Thank you,' she said. 'I will never forget what you did for me today.'

Poppa chose that moment to enter by the French windows, looking like a drowned rat. 'Blimey! No one's answering the front door so I skipped round the back. I've just dropped Jessie off. Anything happen while I was away?'

Tilly giggled for the first time that day, and Hettie—retrieving the three slices of chocolate cake from the table by the French doors and eyeing up the scissors in the window box—smiled. 'I think we can honestly say that peace has finally descended on Furcross, the home for slightly older cats,' she said. 'Shall we pick up some fish and chips on the way home? My shout.'

Mandy Morton began her professional life as a musician. More recently, she has worked as a freelance arts journalist for national and local radio. She currently presents the radio arts magazine *The Eclectic Light Show* and lives with her partner, who is also a crime writer, in Cambridge and Cornwall, where there is always a place for an ageing long haired tabby cat.

Twitter: @icloudmandy, @hettiebagshot
Facebook: HettieBagshotMysteries

Center Point Large Print
600 Brooks Road / PO Box 1
Thorndike, ME 04986-0001 USA

(207) 568-3717

US & Canada:
1 800 929-9108
www.centerpointlargeprint.com